Praise for #1 *New York Times* Bestselling Author Sandra Brown

"Author Sandra Brown proves herself top-notch."
—**Associated Press**

"Brown's storytelling gift is surprisingly rare, even among crowd pleasers."
—*Toronto Sun*

"A master storyteller."
—*Newport News Daily Press*

"Brown's forte is devising plots spiced with sexuality that keep her readers guessing."
—*Library Journal*

"Sandra Brown has continued to grow with every novel."
—*Dallas Morning News*

"Brown truly delivers the goods."
—*Salisbury Post*

"Plotting and pacing are Brown's considerable strengths."
—*San Jose Mercury News*

"She knows how to keep the tension high and the plot twisting and turn

—*F

By Sandra Brown

SANDRA BROWN

WORDS OF SILK

WARNER BOOKS

NEW YORK   BOSTON

Copyright © 1984 by Erin St. Claire

All rights reserved. No part of this book may be reproduced in any form or by any electronic or mechanical means, including information storage and retrieval systems, without permission in writing from the publisher, except by a reviewer who may quote brief passages in a review.

Warner Books

Time Warner Book Group
1271 Avenue of the Americas, New York, NY 10020
Visit our Web site at www.twbookmark.com

Cover design by Jackie Merri Meyer and Gizelle Ferrer
Photograph by Johner/Photonica

Printed in the United States of America

Originally published in hardcover by Warner Books

First Paperback Printing: April 2005

10 9 8 7 6 5 4 3 2 1

To my four sisters—
Melanie, Jo, Lauri, and Jenni—
each beautiful in her own special way

Dear Reader,

For years before I began writing general fiction, I wrote genre romances. *Words of Silk* was originally published about twenty years ago.

This story reflects the trends and attitudes that were popular at that time, but its themes are eternal and universal. As in all romance fiction, the plot revolves around star-crossed lovers. There are moments of passion, anguish, and tenderness—all integral facets of falling in love.

I very much enjoyed writing romances. They're optimistic in orientation and have a charm unique to any other form of fiction. If this is your first taste of it, please enjoy.

Sandra Brown

WORDS
OF SILK

CHAPTER | 1

The elevator was between floors when it came to a jaw-jolting stop and the lights blinked out. There had been no warning, no grinding down of gears, no forecasting flicker of the lights. Nothing. One minute the cubicle had been moving on its silent descent, the next, its two occupants were engulfed in unrelieved black stillness.

"Uh-oh," the man remarked. He was a New Yorker and accustomed to the practical jokes the city played on its citizens. "Another blackout."

Laney McLeod didn't comment. The man obviously expected her to say something. She could *feel* him turn and look toward her. But speech and movement were beyond her. She was paralyzed with fear. She rationalized, telling herself that it was her claustrophobia that made the situation so horrifying, that she would survive, that such stark terror was juvenile and bordered on the ridiculous. It didn't help.

"Are you all right?"

No, I'm not all right, she wanted to scream at him. But her vocal cords were frozen. Eight well-manicured nails were digging into two sweating palms. She realized that her eyes were squeezed shut. But forcing them open made no difference; there was no light in the suffocating confines of the apartment building elevator. Her breath was rasping loudly.

"Don't worry. It won't last long."

His calmness infuriated her. Why wasn't he panicked? She wanted to demand if he could guarantee that the power would be restored shortly. These blackouts could last for days, couldn't they?

"I think I'd feel better if you'd say something. You are all right, aren't you?"

She sensed a hand groping in the darkness only seconds before it made contact with her arm. She jumped.

"It's all right." Quickly he withdrew his hand. "Are you claustrophobic?"

Frantically she nodded her head, illogically thinking he could see the motion. He must have sensed it because his voice took on a lulling inflection. "There's nothing to worry about. If the power isn't restored in a matter of minutes, the fire department will be looking for stranded people like us."

She felt the air stir and heard the soft rustling of clothing. "I'm taking off my coat. I suggest you do the same."

When he had boarded the elevator, she'd gotten only a brief impression of gray hair, a tall frame, a slender physique, and clothes too studiously casual not to be outrageously expensive. Not speaking, not making eye contact, she had watched the lighted numbers over the elevator door as they ticked off their descent.

She had known that he watched her for several moments after he got in, though he hadn't spoken either. They had been subject to that universal awkwardness that comes between two strangers sharing an elevator. Eventually his eyes had joined hers counting down the floors of the building. Now she heard his jacket land on the plush carpet.

"Need any help over there?" he asked with forced cheerfulness when she didn't move. He took a step toward the sound of the heavy, irregular panting and raised his hands. He heard her thump against the paneled wall as she backed away from him. He touched her rigid body and tentatively felt his way to her shoulders. "Hey." His voice was silky soft. "Everything's going to be fine." His hands gave her tense shoulders a reassuring squeeze. Then he moved.

"What are you doing?" Laney hadn't thought she could speak until she heard her own gasped question.

"Helping you off with your coat. The hotter you are, the harder you breathe, and the more likely you may start hyperventilating," he said. "My name's Deke, by the way." The suit jacket she had bought at Saks only the day before was eased off and dropped to the floor. "What's your name? Is this a scarf?"

"Laney." She raised leaden hands and fumbled against his fingers. "Yes. It comes off." She unwound the tie from her neck and handed it to him.

"Laney. That's an unusual name. Maybe you should

unbutton a few buttons too. I don't think your blouse will allow much ventilation. Silk, isn't it?"

"Yes."

"Very pretty too. Blue, if I remember."

"Yes."

"You're not a New Yorker," he remarked casually. He was working at the cuffs of her blouse, unbuttoning the pearl buttons and rolling the sleeves up her arms.

"No. I've been visiting for a week. I'm due to leave in the morning."

"You were visiting someone in the building?"

"Yes. My college roommate and her husband."

"I see. Now, isn't that more comfortable?" He adjusted her opened collar around her throat. "Would you like to sit down?" He lightly touched her waist with both hands.

"No!"

Dammit. Deke Sargent cursed himself for moving too fast. Mustn't panic the panicked. The woman was still plastered against the wall as though she were facing a firing squad. She was breathing as though each inhalation were her last. "All right, Laney. You—"

The lights flickered like a strobe, then came on full strength. The gears of the elevator were engaged with a gentle bump, and they were moving again.

Two strangers stared at close range into each other's eyes. Both pairs were dilated. Her face was pale. His was creased with concern.

He smiled crookedly and returned his hands to her shoulders. She looked ready to fly into a million pieces. "There! See? I told you. Everything's back to normal."

Instead of returning his smile, resuming the aloof detachment of a stranger, thanking him for his patience with her silliness and restoring her clothing, she slumped against him. His shirtfront was clutched in tight, damp fists, and she uttered an anguished cry against his chest. He felt her convulsive trembling.

God bless her, she had forced herself to hold on to her composure as long as she could. But when the danger was over, her nerves had given way to her terror of the dark, confining elevator.

They came to a gliding stop at the lobby level. The door whished open. Through the plate glass windows of the lobby, Deke could see people milling about on the sidewalks. The avenue was thronged with traffic halted by inoperative signal lights. Chaos reigned momentarily.

"Mr. Sargent—" the uniformed doorman began, rushing toward the elevator.

"I'm fine, Joe," Deke said brusquely. The last thing this woman needed was to be thrown out on the street in her condition. He didn't want to make any lengthy explanations to the doorman. "I'm going back up."

"Were you in the elevator when—"

"Yes, but I'm fine."

He propped Laney against the wall and leaned backward to press the Door Close button and the one designating the twenty-second floor. The doors closed and they surged upward. The woman had been impervious to it all. She still slumped bonelessly and hiccupped soft sobs.

"You're all right. You're safe. It's okay," Deke murmured as he held her to him. She smelled very good and he liked the feel of her hair on his neck and chin.

The elevator opened onto the hallway of his floor. Splaying a hand wide over her chest to keep her from collapsing, he bent down to pick up their discarded jackets, the tie of her blouse and her handbag. Then he swept her into his arms and against his chest. He carried her down the hall to the corner apartment and set her gently on her feet.

"Almost there," he whispered as he took his key from his pants pocket and inserted it into the lock. The door swung wide. He scooped the woman in his arms again and strode inside, depositing her on a sofa whose deep cushions almost swallowed her.

When he turned to leave, her arms lifted as though imploring him to stay. "I'll be right back." Unthinkingly he brushed a kiss across her forehead. He hurried back to the door and punched a sequence of numbers on his alarm system, which would have gone off in fifteen seconds had he not. Their clothes and her handbag were retrieved from where he had left them in a pile in the hall. He closed and relocked the door, flipped up a switch that turned on the indirect lighting and adjusted the dimmer down. The room was lit with a suffusion of pale gold.

He crossed the room in three long strides and knelt in front of the sofa, taking her hand between his and chafing it. "Laney?" Her eyes were closed, but they came open at her name. "How are you?"

She looked at him blankly. Two large tears rolled down her cheeks. Then she covered her face with her hands and began to sob. "I was so scared. It's stupid, childish, I know. Claustrophobia . . ."

"Shhh." He got off his knees and sat down beside her. He gathered her in his arms, pressed her face into his neck and stroked her hair. "It's over. All over. You're safe." He kissed her temple. He kissed it again. His hand smoothed down her back and she snuggled closer.

Abruptly he pulled away and cleared his throat roughly. "What you need is a brandy."

He sure as hell needed one. He slowly extricated himself from her clinging hands and went to the small wet bar in the corner. As he poured the aromatic liquor into snifters, he watched her. It was as though her tears had cleansed her not only of panic but of energy too. She had turned sideways on the sofa, tucking her feet beneath her hips and resting her cheek against the back cushion.

Of all the damn things, he thought with a wry smile. Deke Sargent rescuing a woman in an elevator? An absolutely gorgeous woman who had to be helplessly carried into his apartment and was at his mercy? He shook his head as he made his way back to the sofa. No one would ever believe it.

What else could he have done? Turned her out on Manhattan streets in the aftermath of a blackout? But what was he going to do with her?

It never occurred to him to start calling other residents in the building in an attempt to locate the friends she had been visiting. Nor did he examine the possessiveness he felt toward her. He recognized it; he just didn't analyze it. But he thought it had something to do with the sweet curve of her hip as she reclined on his couch and the way her honey-blond hair spilled over the tangerine-colored velvet cushions.

"Here, Laney, drink some of this." He sat beside her again and, cupping her head in his hand, raised the fragile snifter to her even more fragile lips. Her lashes fluttered open. Blue eyes, disoriented but no longer haunted, stared at him for a moment before her lips parted and she took a sip of the finest brandy in the world.

Her face didn't testify to its quality: Her features screwed up comically and Deke chuckled softly as she coughed and sputtered. She wasn't sophisticated, though her well-cut raw-silk suit indicated discriminating taste.

"More?" he asked.

She nodded and surprised him by covering his hand with hers and guiding the snifter back to her mouth. She sipped daintily until most of the brandy was gone. Then she leaned her head against the cushions and sighed deeply. The gesture was innocent, but the swell of her breasts beneath the clinging blouse aroused far from innocent desires in Deke.

Setting her glass on the lacquered coffee table, he drank a long sip of his own brandy. Her condition being what it was, it wasn't fair for him to stare, but he had never professed to being anything but human.

He studied her as she lay against the cushions, head thrown back, throat arched and vulnerable, eyes half closed, lips fragrant and moist with expensive brandy. Her face was too angular to be considered beautiful. The nose was a bit too short. Her mouth . . .

Best not to linger too long in consideration of her mouth.

Her neck was long and slender and showed off delicate collarbones. In the triangle between them beat a steady, if a bit rapid, pulse. Her breasts looked soft, natural, touchable, beneath her blouse, but she was wearing a brassiere. He could see hints of weblike lace and satin straps. Her waist was model-thin. Thighs and hips likewise. From what he had seen of her calves, they were well shaped and encased in pale stockings. His palms itched to stroke them. She was wearing beige suede pumps with a butterfly embossed in shiny thread on the vamp.

Even as he watched, she moved the toe of one shoe to the heel of the other and pushed it off. The other shoe followed. They thumped almost soundlessly to the thick carpet. He dragged his eyes from the slender feet back up to her face. She was watching him with a notable lack of curiosity about her surroundings or about him.

"I couldn't breathe." A row of straight white teeth clamped over the trembling lower lip to still it.

He touched her hair, slid his fingers down her cheek. "That's a terrifying sensation, but it's over now."

"It was so dark." Her frail voice gave out on the last word and she squeezed her eyes shut.

Deke moved quickly to enclose her once again in his arms. "You were frightened. I'm sorry."

Her pliant body conformed to his hard one and mentally he groaned because his responded. Suddenly she was not just a woman who needed comfort and understanding: she was a woman who was soft and feminine and who felt better than any woman he had held recently. He spoke her name aloud.

She raised her head. Her eyes were the color of fog rolling in off the ocean. They were wide and pleading. "Hold me."

"I will," he vowed fervently. She seemed satisfied and nestled her face in his neck. When her lips brushed his skin, he felt the contact all the way down to his manhood. "I'll hold you."

Unconsciously he was raining light kisses over her hair and along her cheek. It seemed natural that he place one finger beneath her chin and tilt her head back. His lips grazed hers lightly before they rested on her mouth. He breathed in the aroma of brandy that lingered on her lips. Only a eunuch could have restrained himself. Deke had never been mistaken as such.

His lips pressed hers. He felt her stiffen momentarily, but then she relaxed against him again. He slowly separated her lips with his tongue and ventured inside. At first his investigation was tentative. When she touched his tongue with hers, his control broke. Making a low growling sound in his throat, he became more aggressive. His tongue claimed the sweet cavern of her mouth for its own, touching everywhere, flicking, stroking.

Her hands knotted handfuls of his shirtfront between clenching fingers. Her legs stretched out over his. She purred. God! Was he having some kind of marvelously erotic dream?

His hand coasted down her front, intending to go around her back for a tighter embrace. But her breast was too much of a temptation and he paused to caress it gently. Regretfully he moved his hand away.

"That felt good. Please do it again."

His head sprang up and Laney was impaled with disbelieving green eyes. The women who usually enjoyed his caresses considered themselves sophisticated. They played at sexual games. Every one had a role and spoke the right dialog. Never had Deke heard such an honest, direct request. It wasn't a demand that he perform a certain act for the sole pleasure of his partner, but a softly whispered compliment on his caress and a plea that he continue it.

He watched her face as his hand slipped back up to her breast. He covered it tenderly and began to rub circles over it. Her eyes closed and she released a long sigh, a slight smile curving her incredible mouth. Daringly he let his fingertips close about the nipple. Even through her blouse and brassiere, he felt its response.

"God, Laney," he whispered thickly before he sealed her mouth with his once again. As the kiss intensified, so did his caresses. He explored her body with an inquisitive hand, finding intriguing curves and hollows, loving the rustling sound of their clothing, which somehow made the caresses seem forbidden and therefore more exciting.

Their position on the sofa frustrated him because his movements were restricted. He rose and pulled her to her feet. She swayed and leaned into him heavily. That brought Deke to his senses. If his body hadn't been raging, he would have laughed at himself and the situation.

She was drunk! And not on spontaneous passion, but on about a cup of brandy. Even residual trauma from the blackout couldn't be responsible for the blank expression on her face.

He sighed, calling himself a fool and willing his ardor to cool. "Come on, Laney, I'm putting you to bed." Hands on her shoulders, he pushed himself away from her. He peered into her face and she solemnly nodded assent. Taking her hand, he headed toward the bedroom. Like an obedient child, she followed.

He switched on the light as they went through the door. "Stand here and I'll turn down the bed." He propped her against the doorjamb and crossed to the wide bed, flinging back the blue suede bedspread, tossing decorative pillows helter-skelter into the deep armchair, plumping a pillow for her and smoothing the flawless toast-brown sheets. "Here you go. . . ."

The words died on his lips. She was still by the door. A small pile of clothing was forming around her. She had taken off her blouse, her skirt. As he turned around she was stepping out of a half slip. Stupefied, he watched her peel gossamer pantyhose down legs that could have been insured for their shapeliness. Then she faced him wearing only a flimsy excuse for a brassiere and a pair of panties that she could have saved money by not bothering with. Her body was both svelte and voluptuous.

None of his colleagues would have believed that Deke Sargent could be rendered speechless. But he stood like a gaping adolescent seeing his first naked woman. His mouth went dry. He had been with so many unclothed women, he couldn't begin to count them. He had undressed most of them himself. He was deft. He could rid a lady of her clothes before she even knew what he was about. But this woman had so taken him unaware that for a moment he could only stand and gawk. What mystified him most was that she wasn't trying to entice him. She had merely taken off her clothes.

She smiled at him demurely as she walked past him on her way to the bed. She lay down and trustfully rested her cheek against the pillow.

"No one is gonna believe I turned this down," Deke muttered to himself as he went to the bed. He smiled down at her. "Good night, Laney, whoever you are. Sleep well." He kissed her cheek and, straightening, automatically reached for the bedside light switch and turned it off.

"No!" She bolted upright, taking heaving breaths in the sudden darkness. Her flailing arms groped for him.

"I'm sorry," he said, cursing his own stupidity and

sitting down on the bed. His arms went around her and he felt her near nakedness. Every male impulse was instantly aroused.

"Stay with me. You promised," she sobbed. Her arms went around his neck and her breasts flattened against his chest. An image of their ripe fullness and dusky centers was imprinted on his brain. "You said you would hold me."

"Laney," he groaned. His conscience and his body warred. "You don't know—"

"Please."

He let himself lie down beside her. Only for a minute. Only until she drifts off to sleep, he told himself.

But she held him tight against her and her entreaties were soft and urgent, just loud enough to drown out the protests of his conscience. His hands began to caress with a purpose other than comforting. Her skin was warm beneath his fingertips. His mouth found hers in the darkness and fused with it hotly, wetly.

Oh, God.

This was wrong. He didn't know anything about her. She might be married. But he had already checked her finger. She wasn't wearing a ring. That doesn't mean a damn thing, Sargent, he thought.

This could get him into a helluva lot of trouble. Think of the publicity. An enraged husband charging into the apartment at dawn with a SWAT team and photographers.

Warnings were fired at him. Her sweet mouth and the feel of her against him shot them down.

He wasn't above using dirty tricks and machinations to get what he wanted. But he had never taken such blatant advantage of a woman. She was intoxicated and didn't know what she was doing.

He did. And it felt wonderful.

He was a good deal older than she. Fifteen years, maybe.

He would probably burn in hell for this. But what did that matter? He was already on fire.

Laney came awake gradually. She lifted her eyelids once, twice. Yawned. Raised them again lazily.

Then they sprang wide. She was sharing a pillow with a total stranger. The man awoke instantly and whispered to her across the soft linen. "Good morning."

Laney uttered a sharp, startled scream and tried to move away from him. Her legs were tangled with his; her knee—Good Lord! His hand was resting heavily on her breast. She thrashed and kicked until she was able to roll away from him. He stared at her as though she had lost her mind and blinked green eyes that even in her near-hysteria she couldn't fail to notice.

She scrambled to the corner of the bed and huddled, making another trapped-animal sound when she realized she was as naked as he. She clutched the corner of the sheet and hauled it up to her chin.

"Who are you and where am I?" she asked, wide-eyed and breathless. "If you don't give me an explanation immediately, I'm calling the police."

Her threat was laughable and she knew it. She didn't even know where she was, much less where the telephone might be.

"Calm down," he said reasonably, and extended a hand toward her. She flinched and moved farther away from him. He cursed.

"Don't you remember how you got here?"

"No," she said shortly. "I only know I didn't come of my own free will. Who are you?"

He cursed again and rubbed his hand over a broad, hair-matted chest as he stared at her in perplexity. "I was afraid you wouldn't remember. You drank too much brandy."

"Brandy?" She mouthed the word, but nothing came out "You gave me brandy? And what else? Drugs?"

He knew from the rising note of panic in her voice that she was about to lose her last vestige of control. "Let me explain."

"Now! Explain now! And where are my clothes?"

He flung back the sheet and got up. She went pale at the sight of all his male power. He took two steps toward a wall of closets before she made another horrified sound. She clamped her hand over her mouth to stifle a full-fledged scream as she stared at the brownish-red stains on the sheets.

She raised glazed eyes to his and for the first time he looked embarrassed. "I didn't know you were a virgin." He spread his arms wide in appeal, seemingly unaware of his bold nakedness. "How could I have known until it was too late, Laney?"

Slowly she lowered a trembling hand from lips gone chalky. "H-how do you know my name?"

He shook his head in what she could only interpret as bewilderment and perhaps a little sadness. He went to the closet and took out a white terry-cloth wrapper and came back toward the bed. He extended the robe toward her. When she didn't reach for it, he laid it down close by her and turned his back. "You told me your name in the elevator. Don't you remember being in the elevator with me?"

She shrugged into the robe and wrapped it around her tightly while he rummaged through a drawer, finally coming up with a pair of pajama bottoms. He pulled them on, but he didn't look like a man accustomed to wearing pajamas.

Facing her again, he asked, "Do you remember getting into the elevator?"

She brought a hand up to her throbbing temple and massaged it, trying to remember. Anything. Yes. She had visited Sally and Jeff last night. Great fun. Sights of New York. A terrific meal and a wonderful drink called a Velvet Hammer for dessert. Two drinks? Then . . . ? Yes. She had said good-bye at their door, hugged Sally, laughingly hugged Jeff; then . . . Nothing.

"You said you were visiting someone who lives in the building," the man prodded quietly, after having given her time to piece together the fragments of memory. "I got on the elevator with you. We had a blackout. We were trapped for several minutes. No more. But you were all undone and I couldn't leave you like that and push you out into the streets. I brought you here. Gave you brandy. I held you while you cried. You—"

"That doesn't explain why I wake up in your bed, having been raped!"

"Raped!" he repeated on a shout of temper.

"Yes, raped. I wouldn't have gone to bed with you willingly."

She watched as he forcefully got hold of his temper. His face was tense with anger and frustration as he looked at her. He ran his hand through his gray hair, beautiful hair that went stunningly well with his darkly tanned skin and startling green eyes. "Did you know you are extremely claustrophobic?" he asked at last.

She nodded tersely.

"I thought you might not remember the sequence of events last night because you were terribly upset." His features softened and she didn't know which frightened her more, his temper or his gentleness. She felt that she could submit to either one.

"As to the other," he added softly and glanced down at the telltale stain on the bed, "I assure you I did nothing you didn't want me to." She whimpered slightly. "I'd like to talk to you about it all. Calmly. Over coffee." He went to a connecting door and opened it. "Here's the bathroom. You might want to shower. I'll bring your clothes in or you can stay in the robe if you don't feel up to dressing. I'll make coffee and slowly we'll put the missing pieces of the puzzle together until it makes sense to you. All right?"

Not all right. But she nodded her consent. He left her

for a moment and came back carrying her hopelessly rumpled clothes, her shoes and her handbag. He said nothing before leaving again and closing the door behind him.

Laney didn't waste time. She bounded off the bed and rushed into the bathroom. She turned on the shower's spray, but she didn't step under it. She only wanted him to think she was in the shower. As much for psychological cleanliness as physical, she washed from the basin.

God! What had she done? One week in New York and she had gotten drunk on a lethal concoction called a Velvet Hammer and gone to bed—to *bed!*—with a total stranger. She couldn't yet grasp the enormity of it.

Her hands were shaking as she pulled on her clothes. Wasting no time, she pulled on her panties, cramming the rest of her underwear into her handbag.

Who was he? She didn't want to know. She would never know.

She opened the door cautiously and peered out. A radio announcer was predicting the weather for the day. A good day for getting the hell out of this city, she thought as she crept toward the front door. She could see his back as he puttered in the kitchen. He seemed not the least upset. Indeed, he had the happily smug bearing of a man who had coerced a woman into his bed and into his shower. Apparently scenes like this morning's weren't infrequent or unfamiliar to him.

Good-bye, Mr. Whoever-You-Are, she mouthed as

she opened the front door and slipped through. She raced on silent feet toward the elevator and pushed the button. It took an interminable amount of time for the car to get to the twenty-second floor and then an even longer time to reach the lobby. Would he notice her absence? Phone down to the doorman and impede her escape?

Laney hurried past the doorman, who bid her a cheerful good morning. She virtually ran two blocks before she even paused to hail a cab. If she wasted no time, she could return to the hotel, pack and still make it to LaGuardia in time to catch her plane.

Her head fell back onto the stiff vinyl seatcover. She experienced a weariness she had never known before. Her body felt sore in new ways she wished she could ignore.

How could it have happened without her even knowing it? She closed her eyes tightly and willed away curiosity. It persisted. He must have been gentle, for surely she would have remembered suffering pain. How had he talked her, Laney McLeod, into making love with him?

"Oh, God," she said, and buried her face in her hands. She didn't know if she was regretting that she couldn't remember it or that she might have to pay severe consequences.

Who was he? He could be married. He could be infected with something. He could be a sexual deviate.

Mirthlessly she laughed to herself. Most women would consider her damned lucky. At least she didn't have to worry about the ultimate horror. Her inability to bear children had been a shield against relationships, a reason for never making a commitment to anyone. She could almost be glad she was barren. She might yet be doomed to suffer some consequences for last night's calamity, but she wouldn't get pregnant.

CHAPTER | 2

"You're pregnant, Ms. McLeod."

Laney stared blankly at the doctor for a moment, then she laughed on a short gust of air. "That's impossible."

He smiled in a kindly, fatherly fashion. "Oh, it's quite possible. I would say you're in your tenth week. Didn't you have an inkling?"

She was shaking her head adamantly, impatiently. "You don't understand. It's impossible. I'm barren. I had appendicitis when I was thirteen. A secondary infection set in and lasted for weeks. The doctor told me and my mother then that I would never be able to have a child."

The doctor shrugged and smiled broadly. "He was wrong!"

"I came in here for a routine stomach virus," she said stridently.

"That stomach malady you suffer from was around

long before we discovered viruses. It's called morning sickness."

Laney became utterly still as she stared at him. He could barely hear her when she said, "You're serious, aren't you? I'm pregnant with a child?"

When he saw the stricken expression on her pale face his tone and manner softened considerably. "Aren't you happy about it, Ms. McLeod?"

Happy? Happy that her sins were finding her out? Happy that she was to pay for one mistake for the rest of her life? Happy that she would make an innocent child pay for her mistake?

"I'm not married," she blurted out. She stood and went to stand at the window. The doctor's office was on the ground floor of a medical complex. People hurried past on the sidewalk. A pickup truck raced through a yellow light. A lady in a station wagon was coaxing a golden retriever to sit down in the backseat. Teenage sweethearts strolled by, their arms around each other's waists.

Normalcy. But nothing was normal. She was pregnant by a man she couldn't even name.

"The father is—" he began.

"Unreachable."

You're very beautiful, Laney.

The doctor coughed lightly behind his hand.

Laney felt like a fool. She could read the doctor's mind. She was rather old to be "getting caught." She had never bothered with contraceptives because she had been under the mistaken impression that she was sterile. Besides, there hadn't been a man until—

"If you make up your mind within a few days," the doctor was saying quietly, "we could terminate the pregnancy. But we don't have much time left."

"An abortion." The whole idea made her shiver with nausea. "No. I don't think so."

I can't believe someone as beautiful and rare as you fell out of the sky into my arms.

"It's not that terrible an ordeal now. We—"

"No," Laney said, spinning away from the window and grabbing up her purse. "I could never do that. Thank you, Doctor," she said hurriedly, desperate now to be alone and to think.

"I'll phone the pharmacy for a prescription of morning-sickness pills and vitamins with iron. You're slightly anemic."

"Thank you." She had almost forgotten what had brought her to see him in the first place—those annoying bouts of queasiness that struck her in the mornings and evenings and that prevailing lack of energy. She had never considered that she could be pregnant. Years ago she had accepted the fact that she would never have a family.

"Check with the receptionist as you leave. Since this is your first pregnancy, I want to see you once a month." The doctor came around the edge of his desk and took her arm kindly. "If there's any way I can help . . ."

He left the offer open-ended. "Thank you," she said, but shook her head no. After making the appointment at the receptionist's desk and accepting the woman's hearty congratulations, she left.

Sunnyvale was having its rush hour, which wasn't an hour at all but lasted from five to five fifteen each workday. It was a bustling community surrounded by a hundred miles of rich farmland. Laney got in her second-hand compact car and drove down the main street. The town boasted most of the nation's fast-food chains, but there was still the Ozark Cafe, where one could eat black-eyed peas and cornbread and homemade banana pudding. There was the obligatory J. C. Penney store, but most of the businesses around the town square were privately owned. Everyone knew everyone else's business.

Everyone knew that the new kindergarten teacher was single. In a few weeks everyone would know she was pregnant.

Laney pulled her car to a stop in the gravel driveway of her rented house and laid her forehead against the steering wheel. "What am I going to do?" she said in anguish.

Touch me.

"I'll lose my job. Then what?"

Oh, God, Laney. That's it, sweetheart. Don't ever be afraid to touch me.

She squeezed her eyes shut and tried not to hear the words. "I could tell them that I was married and lost my husband somehow."

Your breasts are beautiful. Did you know that? Perfect size, shape. Laney, Laney.

"Stop it!" she shouted to the ceiling of her car. Her breath was coming fast. Her upper lip was beaded with perspiration. She covered her breasts with her hands so she wouldn't feel the caressing any longer, wouldn't feel the nipples pouting as though they were being kissed. "Stop it, stop it, please," she moaned.

These snatches of memory had haunted her since the morning almost three months earlier when she had left his apartment building. Like hunters who sensed a weakness in their prey and were closing in for the kill, they revealed themselves more frequently now. They hovered on the outskirts of her mind, popping up from their cover, no longer afraid to be seen. She wouldn't look. She didn't want to remember. God, she didn't want to.

She pushed open the car door and made her way to the front door. The house was old, quaint and small, but she loved it. A foyer opened onto a sunny living room with wide windows. There was a brick fireplace on the far wall. A tiny dining alcove led into a cozy kitchen. On the other side of the house were two bedrooms with a bath between them.

Laney had leased the house on sight with the landlady's permission to make any reasonable changes she wanted to. The first thing she did was hand-wax the hardwood floors, which had been sadly neglected. She painted the rooms bright, cheerful colors and decorated them inexpensively but tastefully.

The only room that still needed her attention was the second bedroom. Maybe she could paint it that weekend. But she should check with the doctor first. Breathing paint fumes would not be good for the baby.

Her hand stilled as she was setting her purse on the entry table. The baby. Had she really thought of it as "the baby?" *Her* baby. Someone to love. Someone to love her.

Suddenly she was laughing and crying at the same time. She *wanted* this baby. Her life wouldn't be so empty then. There would be another person sharing it.

The school board could be convinced to keep her on. And if they couldn't, she would move somewhere else. Nothing was going to interfere with her happiness. She was going to have a baby!

"This is [cough] quite, er, a surprise to say the least, Miss McLeod."

"Ms. McLeod," Laney firmly corrected Mr. Harper. She had asked for a meeting with her principal and the superintendent of schools the morning after she learned of her pregnancy. Best to have the baptism of fire now and get it over with. She was almost three months pregnant. She would begin showing soon. "As I've told you, I'm married but legally separated from my husband. I preferred to use my maiden name after my— our—separation."

The principal looked at the superintendent of schools. He hadn't said a word. The principal mopped his sweating brow. He was the one who had hired Laney McLeod and he was afraid he was going to have to take the blame for this mess.

"And you say now that you're . . . uh . . . going to have a baby?"

Laney moistened her lips. This was the tricky part. How to convince them that she had slept with a husband she was about to separate from. "Yes. I . . . it was one of those . . . we were trying to reconcile," she said with a weak smile. "It didn't work out, but I became pregnant as a result of that weekend."

Now the superintendent began to sweat, too, and he cleared his throat loudly. "I think we understand." He looked at the principal, who wobbled his head in acknowledgment. "What are you asking of us?"

"I want to continue teaching," she said boldly. Better to lay it on the line confidently. "The baby is due in March. That should coincide with the spring break. By that time you will have found a substitute to finish the last eight weeks of school."

Mr. Harper said nothing. He wasn't about to commit himself until the superintendent did.

The superintendent looked at Laney intimidatingly. "This may be awkward. An unmarried kindergarten teacher who is . . . uh . . ."

"Pregnant," Laney supplied. "Yes. I didn't anticipate it happening, either, but that's the way it is. I want to stay on here. The school term has only just started, but I have wonderful projects planned for my students. I love them and they know it. I think they all like me. I have excellent credentials from my job in Tulsa. I can always get a job there." She doubted that but made it sound convincing.

"If you dismissed me, you'd have to find another teacher on short notice. She might not be all that well qualified if she's not teaching already. And even if you did find someone good, in the meantime the curriculum will have suffered." She took a deep breath. "I know this is unorthodox. I understand your position. But I'm a qualified teacher. That should be your first consideration."

As it turned out, it was. She left them alone and ten minutes later they came to her room, where she was pinning Space Shuttle posters on the bulletin board. They were wearing broad, effusive smiles.

"Of course you can stay on, Miss . . . uh, Ms. McLeod," Mr. Harper said, pumping her hand in a wrenching clasp. "If anyone asks, we'll simply tell them what you've told us. You and your husband are temporarily separated."

She was about to correct him on the temporary part but thought better of it. She had gotten this far. If they were optimistically holding out for a nonexistent husband to show up, that was their problem.

The days were getting markedly shorter. By the time she washed her few dinner dishes and went into the living room to stoke the fire in the fireplace, it was dark outside. The two oak trees in her front yard were being lashed by a blustery wind. The weatherman had said the temperature would drop below freezing by morning.

Laney lay down on the sofa and propped her feet on the cushion at the opposite end. It felt good to elevate them. She had to stand most of the day at school. She smiled, running a hand over her burgeoning abdomen. Her students were intrigued by the baby. They asked permission to touch it all the time. Some days, by the time she got home, she had been mauled by thirty pairs of sticky, damp hands. But she loved it. She loved her baby.

There were things she should be doing. A statement from Dr. Taylor had arrived in her mail that day, showing her balance paid in full. That was a mistake that needed straightening out. She still owed him three hundred dollars. But she didn't want to do it tonight. She would call tomorrow. It felt so good not to move.

With a contented sigh she turned her eyes sleepily toward the fireplace. For a moment she held her breath. Something about the light it cast was disturbingly familiar. It was soft, diffuse, golden. Her heart began to pound and she shut her eyes, but the picture was all the more brilliant against her eyelids.

And she remembered it all. The memory came rolling toward her like a giant boulder.

She remembered getting into the elevator and his getting on two floors down. The blackout was just as terrifying in retrospect as it had been in reality, and she heard herself whimper. His soothing voice reached her again through a tunnel of fear. She felt his hands as they gently helped her off with the jacket of her suit, which she had never worn again. She remembered how her buttons had seemed to fall away beneath his dextrous fingers.

His face came into sharp, clear focus as it had when the lights had come on. He was extremely good-looking, and in retrospect she saw that his eyes revealed both shrewd insight and kindness. She might have gone to bed with a stranger, but she didn't have to make an apology for the way he looked.

She saw herself being carried down the hall, saw the room in stark detail. It was decorated in beiges and browns, with the tangerine-colored sofa standing like an island of pleasure in the middle of the room. She saw herself languishing on the incredibly soft cushions, her hair wantonly fanned out behind her, her eyes limpid, her breasts straining against the clinging silk of her blouse.

She could taste the brandy again. And she could taste his mouth, firm and sure, as it moved over hers. She could smell him. He wore a citrusy cologne that was as clean and masculine as he was. In the fantasy his hands were tender as they explored and aroused. She saw herself following him docilely into the bedroom, saw his eyes devouring her as she stood before him virtually naked. She hadn't been ashamed or modest about her body, as she had been taught to be. She had wanted him to look at her and think her beautiful.

The lights went out again and she had reached for him, afraid he would leave her. But he hadn't. He'd come to her, a strong, hard, comforting, sheltering presence lying alongside her, holding her tightly and whispering wonderful things. He kissed her until they were breathless. Her neck and chest were showered with hot random kisses.

Hesitantly he lowered the straps of her brassiere, and when she didn't protest he unsnapped the fastener. He moved the garment aside and brushed her warm, satiny flesh with the backs of his fingers. Curving his palm around her ribs, he placed his thumb in the shallow groove that divided her stomach and drew his hand over her belly, over her navel, to the top of her brief bikini panty. Two of his fingers toyed with the lacy elastic.

"Yes," she breathed.

His hand slid inside and he touched the lush delta of her femininity. "God, you're sweet." His voice had been sandpapery. She lifted her hips to facilitate his taking off the sheer panties. He held her for a long moment close to him, their hearts pulsing together. Then he left the bed only long enough to get out of his clothes. When he drew her close again she uttered a soft moan of pure animal pleasure as his stirring nakedness touched hers.

"Turn the light back on," she had whispered.

"Are you still frightened?"

"No. I want to see you. To see the way we look together."

She could tell that pleased him very much. The lamp bathed them with a magic light that made everything beautiful. Her body was beautiful next to his. He was beautiful, all muscle and sinew and tanned skin dusted with brown hair. Curiously she touched his chest and shoulders and upper arms. "I like the way you look," she had murmured absently.

"Do you?" He had taken her hand, brought it to his lips and lightly licked the tips of her fingers. She had gasped at the shocking pleasure that curled around her insides each time his tongue touched her flesh.

His hands lovingly drifted over her body. They circled her breasts, kneading gently. He cupped her in his palms and rubbed the nipples with his thumbs until she was writhing against him. . . .

"Oh, Deke."

Her eyes flew open. She had spoken his name aloud. Deke. She hadn't allowed herself to remember his name until now. Deke. Why didn't she loathe the name? Why didn't it feel treacherous and hateful and deceitful on her tongue?

She was panting as if she had just run a mile-long race. She didn't want to remember any more, but it was too good a dream to leave unfinished. She closed her eyes again. . . .

"Oh, Deke."

"Your breasts are beautiful. Did you know that? Perfect size, shape. Laney, Laney."

Then his mouth was on her, possessive and gentle at one time. He kissed her ardently, tenderly, adoringly. He teased her nipples with the tip of his tongue, playing it over them again and again until she was conscious of nothing save for the waves of ecstasy that washed over her.

"You taste so good." His lips closed around her and tugged her softly, sweetly, into the heat of his mouth.

He rolled her onto her back and eased himself on top of her. He separated her thighs with his and nestled against her, hard and throbbing. She wasn't afraid. She was yearning.

"I can't believe someone as beautiful and rare as you fell out of the sky into my arms." His lips nibbled the length of her throat and she arched it, giving him access. She lightly ground her hips against his hardness and reveled in his growl of approval. He fastened his mouth to hers in a fiery kiss. His tongue thrust deeply into her mouth.

Laney felt her body opening. Like the moist petals of a flower whose time had come to bloom, her body prepared the way for him. He sensed it. His hand stroked down the outside of her thigh, affectionately squeezed a handful of her fanny, then slipped between her thighs. He caressed her with his fingertips until she was chanting his name and clinging to him with shameless need.

He touched her intimately, acquainting himself with her readiness. His fingers were provocative and bold, yet tender. So tender.

He poured words into her ear, silken words, words that were poetic and sensual, suggestive and explicit, words that made her ashamed, exultantly so.

"Are you sure, Laney? Is there any reason I shouldn't?"

She flung her head from side to side on the pillow. "No. Love me now, Deke. Just love me. Love me."

He introduced his body into hers slowly. He pressed steadily but unhurriedly, as though he wanted to prolong the intense pleasure of total possession.

And then he encountered the barrier of her virginity and he froze. For ponderous seconds he waited. Then he raised his head and stared down at her until her eyes opened. She read in his face intensity and passion, a little anger, much compassion and great regret.

"Why didn't you tell me, Laney?"

Her arms had folded behind his neck and she urged her body upward, wanting him inside her. "I want to be loved. Now please, Deke."

"But—"

"Deke," she cried, and arched against his hips.

She heard his anguished curse. But he couldn't have restrained himself then. No power on earth could have kept him from taking her then. With a steady, unyielding pressure he delved into her body until he was fully imbedded in her snug warmth.

"Oh, God." Anguish and ecstasy went into his soft cry. "Are you in pain, Laney? Did I hurt you?"

"No," she sobbed on tears of happiness. "No."

"You feel so good, so right," he whispered into her neck. "Tell me if I hurt you."

But he didn't. Not that time or the time after, when he hadn't wanted to for fear it would be too much. She had begged him, and when he still refused, she had made it physically impossible for him to say no. He entered her again and again that night, and each time was better than the last, each stroke more delicious than the last. And each time he had brought her to a crashing climax, only to let her glide peacefully back into his loving embrace.

Now Laney opened her eyes and let go a pent-up sigh. "Good Lord." She remembered everything, every outrageous thing she had done and every outrageous thing she had said, things she would have never imagined herself capable of saying and doing. The words he had used to describe her, their lovemaking, their bodies, flowed over her again in scalding memories. Her hands covered her face while she tried to eradicate the erotic pictures that flashed through her mind. She felt feverish, and her body was trembling so violently, she could hardly stand.

She went into the bathroom and let cold water trickle over her wrists. She rinsed her face with handfuls of it. Her mirror reflected the same face she had known for years, but she knew that after that night she would never be the same.

Now she knew why people were so absorbed by sex. Now she knew what all the joking in the teachers' lounge was about.

"Oh, you poor thing," they had said when she had made her announcement.

"You mean the jerk got you pregnant just before you split up?"

She had turned her back to pour a cup of coffee. "It's not so bad. Really. I always wanted a baby." They seemed not to hear.

"Just like a man."

"Yeah. He'll say and do anything to get you in bed with him, but it's kaput the next day." This was from one woman who was divorced but constantly looking for a new partner. She had grinned and stretched indolently in the cracked vinyl chair. "Still, it's good while it lasts, isn't it?" They had all laughed. Laney had forced a smile.

Now she had to admit that yes, it had been good while it lasted. Better than good. It had been the most wonderful thing that had ever happened to her. She had never thought it would. It never would again. She couldn't feel ashamed about it, because out of that night had come her baby. She placed her hands on her stomach now and patted it. "I'll love you so much."

It occurred to her that she didn't even know Deke's last name. He would never know he had a child and it was just as well. He wouldn't have cared. He had probably forgotten all about that night by now. A man who looked like that, lived in that luxurious apartment, wouldn't ever be without a woman. She still had no guarantee that he wasn't married.

Laney paled at the thought, but in thinking about it, she doubted that he was. That hadn't been a couple's bedroom. The apartment was blatantly masculine, without a trace of femininity. No, he couldn't have been married.

She had been unfair to him the following morning. He had taken advantage of her unstable condition. That was indisputable. But he had also been telling the truth. He hadn't done anything she hadn't wanted him to do. She had clutched at him, begging him to make love to her.

Why had she behaved that way? Had he been that seductive? Or had she wanted to be held so badly that anyone would have done? She doubted that too. They said that even under hypnosis a person couldn't be made to do something he didn't subconsciously want to do.

So, by deductive reasoning, this was fact: She had wanted to make love to that man and had used her hysteria and tipsiness as an excuse.

It meant nothing to either of us, she told herself. A

biological transfer. That's all. It was a means of getting a baby you never expected to have. For that reason you can't regret it, but you don't have to dwell on it. Think of the baby as a gift. Accept it and forget the other.

But she couldn't.

Touch me.

Her fingers had dusted the body hair on his chest. It tapered to a sleek line down his flat, taut stomach.

Touch me. Oh, God, Laney.

He was hard and warm and full with life ready to burst free.

That's it, sweetheart, that's it. Don't ever be afraid to touch me. Touch me, touch me, touch me . . .

"I want to touch it."

"No, me."

"It's moving!"

"Is not."

"Is too. Isn't it moving, Miss McLeod?"

Patiently, Laney gently pushed the too-eager hands away from her abdomen. "Yes, it's moving, and I think it's had enough of this handling." The dozen or so children crowding around her and stepping on her black suede boots protested whiningly. "Besides," she said, raising her voice over the grumblings, "recess is over and we need to get inside. Remember that after lunch we're going to assemble our Christmas stockings."

"It's not fair. I didn't get to touch the baby," another complained as Laney organized them into two reasonably straight lines.

"Tomorrow, maybe," she said absently, counting heads.

"I want to touch the baby too."

Laney froze. How she recognized the voice, she didn't know. It had been over six months since that night in New York. But she knew instantly who had come up behind her, taking her completely unaware.

When she turned around, he was smiling, standing only a foot away, looking hilariously out of place in the schoolyard. He was wearing an expensive overcoat of a gray-green wool that did marvelous things for his coloring. The collar was turned up to perfectly frame a rawly appealing masculine face and wind-tossed gray hair.

"You look beautiful, darling," he said.

And while Laney stood as immobile as a mannequin, he stepped forward, cupped her cold cheeks between his warm palms and kissed her.

CHAPTER | 3

The kiss was warm, chaste and infinitely tender. When he pulled away, his eyes were twinkling with mischief and delight over her mute surprise. The children had gone wild, giggling and whooping because their Miss McLeod had been kissed.

When he finally dropped his hands from her cheeks, Laney took a step back and said, "What do you think—"

"Well, I see you found her." Mr. Harper was huffing toward them, his face wreathed in smiles and relief. "She was right where I said she'd be, wasn't she, Mr. Sargent?"

Sargent. Deke Sargent.

"Yes, she was."

Though he answered the principal, Deke continued to stare at Laney hungrily. She tore her eyes away from that ravenous gaze and addressed Mr. Harper. "And just why was Mr. Sargent looking for me?"

Could she brazen this out? Could she act as though she didn't recognize or remember him? It was worth a try.

"Easy, Laney," he muttered under his breath.

"Well . . . well, of course he was looking for you," Mr. Harper stammered. "Your husband came to the office and told me that you two had reconciled. We're all very glad to hear that. And just in time for Christmas!" He chuckled and folded his hands across his stomach, beaming at them.

"That's Miss McLeod's husband," one of the children piped up.

"She's not married or she would be Mrs. not Miss."

"She's Ms., stupid, don't you know anything? And of course she's married 'cause she's gonna have a baby."

"Yeah, my mom said you have to be married before you can have a baby."

"Do not."

"Do too."

"Husband?" Laney squeaked, turning away from the children.

Mr. Harper laughed. "I see you haven't gotten used to having him around again."

"She'll get used to it," Deke said silkily. "Darling, I think the children are getting cold. By the way, did someone mention lunch? What's on the menu today?"

"Pizza," said one of the children.

"And salad."

"But no free ice cream."

Deke smiled down into thirty openly curious faces. "Wha'd'ya say I buy ice cream for everyone today?"

That was the proverbial straw. The children went crazy. They fractured the haphazard lines Laney had urged them to form, and eddied around her en masse. She stood rooted to the playground, feeling the foundations of her life slowly crumbling and knowing she was helpless to stop the erosion.

"Children, children, remember not to run," Mr. Harper said, chasing after them as they swarmed toward the door. "Walk, please."

"Let's get in out of this wind, Laney. I'd hate for you to catch a chill."

She stared, dumbfounded, as Deke took her elbow and began escorting her back toward the building. If she hadn't been so livid, she probably would have laughed at the farce that was being played out. She yanked her arm free.

"I don't know what you're trying to pull, but—"

"But you'd better go along with it, because Mr. Harper is thrilled that we're back together." His dazzling smile belied the tense undercurrents in his voice.

She glanced toward the door. The children had filed through. The principal was holding the heavy door for them and grinning stupidly. She wanted to slap him. She wanted to stamp and scream and tear at her hair. But she had learned early on to keep every emotion well under control. One didn't make a fool of oneself by displaying what one was feeling, so she only glowered at Deke Sargent.

"You won't get away with this," she said out of the corner of her mouth.

He took her hand and linked their fingers. "I already have." Short of causing a big scene with Mr. Harper looking on, she had no choice but to go with him through the door and rejoin the class.

The rest of the day was like a bad script. A parody. A comedy in which everyone but she knew their lines. She groped and grappled for rational things to say when nothing made any sense.

Sitting across from her at lunch in a cafeteria full of squirming, noisy children was the man who stocked expensive brandy and owned a signed and numbered artwork by Leroy Neiman. It made her distinctly uncomfortable that she could remember the lithograph in such detail. It had hung over the marble fireplace.

He ate the rubbery slice of pizza and the soggy salad as if it were haute cuisine at 21. He smiled at her across the stained Formica table lined with plastic trays and water-spotted stainless. Standing like sad sentinels down the center of the table were bottles of artificial sweetener, stopped-up salt shakers and broken paper-napkin dispensers. Yet, he seemed perfectly at home.

He touched her, frequently. He fetched and carried and anticipated her every need until she thought she would scream. Only the presence of the other teachers, observing like dreamy-eyed sorority girls, prevented her from dumping his tray in his lap just to see how much he would smile then.

"My God," someone hissed in her ear, "have you lost your mind?"

WORDS OF SILK   45

"Huh?" Laney turned around to see two of the most dedicated men-chasers on the staff gazing at Deke as he passed out the ice-cream bars he had bought for her classroom.

"You let him get away? Even for a little while?"

"Honey, I'd put up with wife-beating to keep him in my bed."

"He's a hunk. An absolute hunk."

"Why in the world would you have ever left him? I'd have gone crawling back."

Laney had passed the boiling point a long time ago. Would they believe the truth? "The first time I met him I was stuck in an elevator and hysterical. He took me to his apartment, plied me with brandy, got me drunk and took full advantage by stripping us both naked, getting into bed with me and making love to me all night."

They looked at her as though she were mentally deranged. "That's bad?" they chorused.

Her students were unruly all afternoon, excited by the holiday season and the appearance of a man who, in their estimation, rivaled the most dashing heroes of their favorite television shows. By the time the final bell rang, Laney was physically exhausted, mentally drained and emotionally shredded.

Why was he there? Why had he come looking for her?

"Ready, darling?"

"I am not your darling!" She had been needlessly straightening papers on her desk until the last child left the room. Now she whirled around to face him and unleashed the fury that had been building all day. "Stop

calling me that. Stop calling me anything. And why are
you here? How did you find me and what do you want?
I want an explanation, dammit!"

"So do I!" he shot back.

His flare of temper startled her and she retreated into
hostile silence as she tossed things into her book bag.
He was holding her coat. There was nothing to do but
to let him help her with it. He buttoned it to the top button, daring her to protest as he fixed her eyes with his.
She picked up her purse and together they left the room
and walked down the vacant hallway, which smelled of
paste, crayons, Christmas peppermint and sweaty wool.

Once outside she headed for the parking lot. Parked
beside her battered compact was a sleek brown Cadillac. No puzzle whom it belonged to.

"I owe you nothing, Mr. Sargent. Not an explanation. Nothing. You wasted your time in coming here
and I'll thank you not to bother me again." While she
had been delivering that brilliant exit line, she had been
unlocking her car door. Now she faced him with cool
condescension.

He was smiling. "I'll see you at home." He pecked
her lightly on her cold, stiff cheek and circled her car to
get into his. He hauled the door open, but before stepping inside, he said, "By the way, Laney, don't bother
trying to lose me. I know where the house is."

She cursed as she slammed the car door, cursed the
cold motor—which took an inordinate amount of time
to start, while the Cadillac's engine growled power-
fully—cursed the school bus she got caught behind in

traffic, cursed the man who was going to ruin her life, such as it was.

He turned his car in behind hers and somehow beat her to the front porch. She watched with horror as he extracted a key from his coat pocket and unlocked the door. "Where did you get that?" she demanded from the lowest step on the porch.

"Come inside, Laney, it's cold."

"Answer me! Where did you get a key to my house? And I'll be damned if I'm going into that house alone with you."

He sighed in exasperation and took the steps down to reach her. "I feel a scene coming on. Would you rather have it out here on the front lawn? KINDER-GARTEN TEACHER HUSTLED ON FRONT LAWN BY RABID NEW YORKER. Is that how you want tomorrow's head-lines to read? Or do you want to be reasonable and get your sweet tush through that damn door before I bodily carry you in?"

He had made his point. She stalked past him but came to an abrupt halt just inside the door. Two suit-cases stood in the middle of the living-room floor. There was an all-weather coat hanging on her brass coat tree. A racquetball racket was leaning against the leg of the sofa. A briefcase was lying on the coffee table.

Shaking with fury, she slowly turned on him. "Col-lect your things and get out of my house."

"*My* house." He fished in his pocket and took out a receipt, which he waved in front of her eyes. "Your lease was only for six months. Remind me to advise you on such matters, Laney. Anyway, it was going to expire next month. I paid this month's rent, signed a new lease—for six months, because by that time the baby will be here and we'll need more room—and paid the full amount of rent in advance. Now, legally you could kick me out for the next month, until you've fulfilled your lease, but I checked with the utility company and your bill was two months old, so I paid it. Also water, telephone and sanitation. I think that entitles me to one month's lodging."

She watched his mouth and was stunned by the words she heard spilling out of it. "You're crazy and I'm calling the police." She spun away from him and barreled toward the telephone, but he merely shrugged out of his overcoat and hung it on the coat tree.

"And tell them what? That your husband is now living in your house with you?"

"You're not my husband!"

He held up his index finger. "*But* everyone thinks I am. You spun the lie about being legally separated from your husband, Laney. I'm only covering for you."

"How did you know about that?" She gripped the back of a chair for support.

His smile would have melted an iceberg. "I've spent six months looking for you. There's little I don't know."

"Well, I don't know anything about you except that your gall is unbelievable and that you're insane if you think you can barge in on me like this and get away with it." She drew a deep breath and said with what she hoped was level firmness, "I want you out of here. Now."

A hint of temper lit the green eyes again. "You have something that belongs to me. Something that I want very much." His eyes dropped significantly to her stomach.

Instinctively her hands covered it. "No," she whispered. Then she repeated fiercely, "No!"

He took a step toward her and she cringed. His anger erupted. "Get out from behind that goddamn chair, Laney. Don't ever cower from me like that. My God, the last thing I would do is hurt you."

She didn't move, and he went toward her and gently but firmly took her arm. "Come sit in the kitchen while I fix you something hot to drink. You look exhausted." He eased off her coat and flung it negligently on the sofa. "Those kids of yours are terrific, but how you stand that pandemonium every day, I'll never know."

Obediently, mindlessly, Laney let herself be led into the kitchen. She didn't object because she was too exhausted to voice a complaint, and because she was too confused to think, and because his hand felt strong and warm and solid and supportive against the aching small of her back.

"What have we got?" he said, checking out the contents of the pantry. "I think I'll have to make a run for groceries. How about hot chocolate?" He had found two packages of hot chocolate mix and was now filling her kettle and turning on the burner of the range as though he did that every afternoon at three thirty when she came in from school.

"Why are you doing this?" She sounded like a parrot, tiredly repeating the same question.

He set two mugs on the countertop and turned around, looking at her for a long, silent moment. Finally he said, "That should be obvious, Laney. I want you and I want my baby." She paled and swayed slightly. He lunged toward her and placed his hands on her shoulders. "Please sit down before you drop."

He gently pushed her into the chair, and when her head fell forward to rest on the backs of her hands on the table, he massaged the top of her head. "Your hair has grown longer."

"I haven't found anyone here to cut it." She couldn't believe she was carrying on this ordinary conversation when there were so many holes she needed to fill with information.

"It's very pretty. I like it longer. More to run my fingers through." His fingers threaded through her hair caressingly. "I guess you couldn't bring your hairstylist with you when you moved from Tulsa."

Her head came up then and she stared at him. He answered her unspoken question. "Yes, I know that you moved here shortly after your vacation to New York."

"How did you find me?"

He went to the stove to pour the now boiling water into the mugs and stirred the hot chocolate until it foamed on the top. He placed one mug in front of her; then, taking up his own, he propped his hips against the counter and crossed his ankles in front of him. His trim, long legs were clothed by camel-colored designer slacks. He was wearing a V-necked navy cashmere sweater over a discreetly plaid cotton shirt. Hand-stitched brown Italian loafers were on his feet. His hair was attractively windblown. He was lean and hard and fearsomely male, yet the caress from his eyes was pure velvet.

"I'm an attorney. A criminal-defense attorney. Once I located Sally and Jeff James after they returned from their trip to England . . ."

He paused and she filled in the gaps. "They were going to leave the day after . . . after I saw them. Jeff is a teacher. He was going to Oxford for two months of research."

"After you left that morning, I nearly tore the building up looking for the friends you had told me you spent the evening with. I must have just missed them. No one I grilled had had a guest named Laney visiting the night before. I checked with the doorman about all the people living in the building who were out of town. He gave me their name after I told him why I needed the information. He remembered your leaving that morning. He didn't blame me for wanting to find you."

She took another drink of chocolate and stared out the window, hoping she looked unimpressed by all he was telling her. Actually her heart was thumping as much as the baby, who seemed to recognize the low, resonant voice of his father and was bouncingly cele-brating his arrival.

"It took weeks for me to make connections with them. I was involved in a case and they were touring the English countryside." He ran a hand through his hair and sipped at his mug of chocolate. "Anyway, we finally made contact."

"You didn't tell them—"

"No," he said softly, shaking his head. "I told them I had found a credit card belonging to you in the elevator and asked them for your mailing address. They gave me the one in Tulsa."

"But by that time I had already moved."

"Yes," he said grimly. "You had closed up the house and arranged to have your mail held in Tulsa until you provided the post office with a forwarding address."

"When I eventually sent for my mail, you found me."

"No. I found you before that."

"How?"

He grinned devilishly. "In all modesty I have a well-known practice in New York," he said with a sweeping bow. "I have access to records, files, law enforcement agencies. You were . . . located." He came to the small round table and pulled a chair close to hers until their knees were touching.

"I was in the middle of a trial and couldn't leave, but I had people reporting in—"

"You had me spied on!" She was furious and tried to bolt out of the chair, but he grabbed her hands and held her down.

"Don't think of it that way."

"That's the only way to think of it. God! Wasn't violating my body enough for you? Did you have to violate my privacy too?"

It took an act of will for him to curb his temper.

"Will you please calm down, Laney? High blood pressure can't be good for the baby."

"I'll worry about the baby. And you can go to hell." She thrust his hands aside and stood, but he sprang up beside her and caught her shoulders—not painfully, but with enough authority to keep her from moving.

"Sit down," he said. When she didn't comply, but only shifted her shoulders beneath his hands, he said with more force, "Laney, sit down."

Because she wasn't about to strain herself and the baby with a tussle she couldn't possibly win, she sat. He resumed his chair. "By the way, I like that dress. Pregnancy suits you."

She looked at him in stupefaction. One minute he was issuing orders like a prison warden, then he was complimenting her on her dress. Her dress? She looked down at the plain red wool jumper. Under it she wore a white blouse with a black grosgrain tie. If it hadn't been for her burgeoning stomach, she might have been a parochial schoolgirl.

She didn't thank him for the compliment. She didn't say anything; instead she stared at him with all the animosity she felt for him. Any moment now she was going to have to get tough and throw him out. Where she would get the energy and the wherewithal, she didn't know.

"When I learned you were pregnant, I wrapped up the trial as quickly as I could."

"Not at the expense of your client, I hope," she said, sarcasm dripping from her lips.

"Of course not," he snapped. "He was given probation."

"For what?"

"Armed robbery."

She sneered at him. "I don't like you, Mr. Sargent. Or your insufferable arrogance. Or even what you do for a living. Doesn't it prick your conscience to send hardened criminals back onto the streets to strike innocent citizens again?"

His eyes went cold for a second and his lips thinned in irritation, then he said calmly, "He wasn't a hardened criminal. He was eighteen years old and his father had abused him and his mother since he was born. He had held up a liquor store in order to buy her medicine."

That took the wind out of her sails. She licked her lips nervously as she dropped her eyes from the penetrating power of his. "Oh," she said in a small voice. But she wasn't ready to surrender yet. "But you were well paid to defend him."

"I was court-appointed."

Damn! Was the man a saint? Didn't he have one flaw? Yes, he seduced women ruthlessly, without one glimmer of remorse or a shred of guilt. "But you've been well paid before. You've gotten people off when you knew they were guilty."

"Yes," he admitted levelly. "It's not my job to judge them. It's my job to defend them to the best of my ability."

He was so cool and collected, while she felt as if the elements of her life were scattering like the fallen leaves tumbling in the December wind outside. Physically she couldn't combat him. Persuasion was the only weapon left to her. "You have no right to bulldoze your way into my life."

"I feel I do. After that night this summer."

"That was an accident. A freak incident. I didn't know what I was doing."

"Didn't you?"

"No! You took unfair advantage. I didn't even remember the details of what had happened until months later."

Knowing she was telling the truth, he pondered that for a moment, then asked, "What did you think about it when you remembered?"

"I was horrified."

"By me?"

"By *me*. I don't want to talk about it."

"I do. What did you think about our lovemaking?"

She shuddered. Was it out of revulsion or remembrance of his hands, his lips, his tongue? She drew in a gulp of air. "It was appalling."

"It was beautiful. You were beautiful. Why do you say it was horrifying and appalling, Laney?"

"I'm not in your courtroom, counselor. Stop cross-examining me."

"Your breasts are larger."

"What?"

He leaned forward and cupped one breast with his hand. She was too dismayed to react, but only sat there and watched as his hand moved lightly over her full breasts. He gently fondled one, then the other.

"They've gotten larger with the baby. Are you going to breast-feed?"

She grabbed his wrist, which was encircled by an eighteen-carat-gold watch, and shoved his hand away. Her breathing was rapid and shallow, and she didn't know if it was because she was outraged at his touching her or because his caress had felt so good. Her breasts were fuller with the new life she carried. And much more sensitive.

She wanted to smash his confidence, offend him, hurt him. "The baby or how it will be fed is none of your business. It isn't yours."

For a moment he remained speechless and she took the opportunity to stand and go to the sink. She rinsed out her mug and then turned to him with smug triumph.

He burst into hearty laughter. For long moments it echoed off the walls of her small kitchen. With his laughter Laney's rage increased. She clenched her fists. "What are you laughing at?"

"You," he said, grinning up at her. "You're priceless, wonderful." He studied her in sheer delight, then his eyes grew serious as he gazed into hers. "Laney, you were a virgin the night we were together."

She licked her lips rapidly and her mind spun crazily. "There was a man in Tulsa. We had been seeing each other for a long time. He wanted to marry me. After New York, I felt terrible about what I had done and—"

"And you slept with him out of guilt."

"Yes, yes, several times before I moved here."

"Why aren't you together now? Where is he?"

Where is he? "He was disillusioned to find out that I wasn't . . . that I had—"

"Been with another man."

"Yes," she agreed readily, getting into the spirit of her lie. "You ruined that for me too."

"So, because you had been with me first, he decided, after all those times you slept with him, that he couldn't stand the thought of your having slept with another man and dumped you." He ticked the points off on his fingers as though trying to arrange them in logical order. "Even though you were carrying his child?"

"I really can't blame him."

Deke barely contained his laughter. "I think he's a damn fool."

"Well, you would! Because you don't know the first thing about decency and honor."

"Apparently you don't either. There's no decency and honor in lying, Laney. That's not only a bald-faced lie, it's a badly constructed one. I know a lie when I hear one. Remember, it's my business to spot them." He placed his thumbs together and extended his arms, framing her stomach between his outstretched hands. Cocking his head to one side and squinting one eye, he said, "That's my child, all right. I think he even looks like me already." He was laughing.

"I tell you, the baby isn't yours," she fairly screamed.

He was unperturbed. "Then I'll just wait around until it's born and we'll know by the birth date, won't we?"

Her shoulders heaved in anger and her face wrinkled

in frustration. "Don't, darling. Don't get so upset." He reached out and caught her around the waist, pulling her between his wide-spread knees. One hand splayed over the small of her back, the other spread over her swollen abdomen. He rubbed his palm over her in soothing circles.

"This is my child, Laney. I know it. I mean to have him and I mean to have you."

"You can't have either." She hated the note of desperation she heard in her voice.

"I do," he whispered. "Right here in my hands." He nuzzled her stomach with his nose and mouth, brushing ardent kisses into the material of her dress. Through the fabric she felt them. They made her insides flutter. "You won't have to bear it alone from now on. I'll be with you."

Almost lulled by his caressing, she suddenly caught his hair between her fingers and brought his head up. "You can't mean that you intend to stay. In this town?"

He smiled a smile that was coming to be familiar. A naughty-little-boy smile. "In this *house*. I'll admit Main Street in Sunnyvale isn't exactly Fifth Avenue, New York, but I think it's a rather quaint place. Middle American. Wholesome. For the time being, this is our home."

"But you can't." She struggled with her thoughts. None of this was possible, yet it was happening. This cosmopolitan man was crowding into her small niche on the planet and she wasn't prepared to cope with his intrusion or the way she felt about it. "We can't live together. What will people think?"

He laughed. "They think we're married, remember?"

"I'll tell them we're not." The moment the defiant words left her mouth, she saw the trap she'd caught herself in. He apparently, by his sly grin, had already thought of that.

"Then you'll be truly offending their sensibilities, won't you? Because you'll be confessing to having a child out of wedlock. Not to mention lying and making fools of them all." He made a *tsk*ing sound with his mouth. "I don't think Mr. Harper would like that."

Neither did she. Her job was more important now than ever. She couldn't risk losing it just before her child was to be born. How would she support him? "I'll tell them that we tried to mend our differences but that they were irreconcilable."

"And I'll say the opposite."

A groan issued from her throat. At first she thought the sound was one of frustration and helplessness. But it may have been generated by pleasure. His hands were massaging the base of her spine and he had rested his cheek on her stomach.

At that moment the baby moved. It was a swift, sudden kick.

Deke jerked his head up, looking first at her stomach, then at her face. "The baby?" he whispered, as though he might disturb it.

She nodded dumbly, anger and frustration suspended for the moment. The high emotion that overrode his features clogged her throat and glossed her eyes with tears. The result of their night together was a bond neither could deny. The miracle of it swamped everything else. "Yes."

"I still can't believe it." He kissed the spot on her stomach, then brought his hands around and completely covered the maternal mound protectively. He lifted his head and looked at her once again as his hands glided up her body, over her breasts, and came to rest on either side of her neck as he stood. "Laney."

He kissed her. This kiss was just as sweet and tender as the one in the schoolyard. But this one had an added element. Passion—passion held prisoner for hours but now unbound.

His lips were warm as they covered hers. They were persuasive, but brooked no argument to his right to kiss her. He ignored the tension that spiraled through her body and stiffened her muscles, ignored her attempts to draw away, ignored her firmly set mouth. His tongue flicked the corners of her lips mercilessly, relentlessly, until they parted. Lazily he sampled the sweet lining, then pressed his tongue deep.

Her whole body went limp under the onslaught and he sighed in supreme satisfaction when he felt her body's response. "Laney," he sighed as his arms went around her and he hauled her close.

The scent of his cologne filled her nose, her head. She remembered the feel of him, the texture of his hair as her fingers clutched at his nape. The taste of his mouth was one she would never forget, and as his kiss intensified, she relished the flavor of him.

At long last he pulled away and smoothed mussed strands of hair from her flushed cheeks. He kissed the tip of her nose. She watched him through a haze of sensuality, her whole body tingling with aroused senses that had long been asleep.

"Do you want to take a nap or go into town and do some shopping with me?"

"Town? Shopping? What for?"

"A king-size bed. I may hurt you if we share that double."

CHAPTER 4

The words were like a bucket of ice water thrown in her face to shock her out of her daze. She pushed herself away from him and sailed through the door into the living room. The racquetball racket offended her most of all. It, more than pajamas and toothbrush, hinted at permanence. She picked it up and flourished it in his face.

"You cannot just move into my house and into my life this way. Please leave."

He was taking his coat from the coat tree and slipping it on. "Do you play racquetball? After the baby comes, we could have fun playing together." His green eyes were dancing.

"Don't you hear me?"

Impatiently he sighed. "Yes, I hear you, Laney." He went to the door. "I think a nap would be better for your bad mood than a shopping trip. I'm going to the furniture store and then to the supermarket. Go lie down."

He held up his key. "I won't even have to disturb you when I come in. I have my key. By the way, you have the most erotic mouth." His voice took on a gravelly pitch and his eyes narrowed. "Do you remember everything," he stressed the word, "we did that night?"

"No."

The hot color that flooded her cheeks was a dead giveaway to her lie. He smiled lazily. "Yes, you do. And so do I." He flipped up the lock, blew her a kiss and left, quickly closing the door against the cold wind.

Laney stood in the middle of the living-room floor, still foolishly brandishing the racket. As though it weighed a thousand pounds, she let her arms drop to her sides. Never had she felt so defeated. What was she going to do? Covering her eyes with her hands, she made her way blindly toward her bedroom. She barked her shin on one of the suitcases standing in the middle of the floor and kicked it viciously, sending it sliding across the hardwood floor toward the fireplace.

"Damn him!" she cursed. Tears blurred her eyes. Her whole body felt clumsy and heavy and tight. Her clothes were restricting. She had never been so tired, physically and emotionally. She felt that she had been on the rack all day and that her bones and her spirit were about to break with the final turn of the crank.

But she knew she couldn't break. If she gave him an inch, he would take a mile. Two miles. As soon as he got back she would pack him up and send him on his way. Somehow. Only she was too tired to think of a plan now.

She peeled off her clothes and let them fall where

they might as she dragged her feet toward the bed. She collapsed on the side of it and barely managed to take off her pantyhose before falling back onto the pillows and pulling the bedspread over herself.

She would rest for just a while. Then she would carry his belongings out to the front porch and call the police if necessary to keep him out. The project sounded exhausting. But she would feel better and have more energy as soon as she rested.

"How can you sleep with all that activity going on?" The low voice gently beckoned her from a deep sleep.

"Hm?" she murmured, yawning broadly. Her eyes remained closed.

"He's kicking up a storm. I think he's hungry for his dinner, even if you're not."

"Dinner?" she repeated drowsily, stretching and rolling slightly to her back. Then her whole body jerked in reaction and her eyes popped open.

Deke was crouched beside the bed. Though she was covered with the bedspread, his hands were beneath it, lying on the naked skin of her abdomen. She had stripped to her brassiere and panties. She could still wear bikinis. They rode just beneath the bulge of her stomach.

"What are you doing?" she asked hoarsely. She was thirsty and her head was buzzing, still muzzy from the depth of her slumber.

"Marveling over the wonder of it all." His hands were soothing on her stretched skin. His fingers pressed into her lightly and he laughed when the baby seemingly did a complete somersault. "What is that little guy doing in there?" His expression and voice were filled with delight.

For a moment Laney was moved by the extent of his apparent joy in the child. But she remembered the resolution she had made before falling asleep and struggled to prop herself up on her elbows. The bedspread slid away and she was left with only her underwear and Deke's hands to cover her.

Dismayed, she looked down to see that her breasts were coming out of her brassiere. She grabbed for the bedspread. Deke was quick to move it out of her reach. "Let me see you. Please." His hands seemed to sift down until she felt their touch.

"Lovely," he murmured as his index finger traced the upper curves swelling over the tenuous border of lace. His touch was feather light, but it sizzled into her and singed each nerve ending. She bit back a gasp of pleasure. Shock rendered her muscles useless as she watched him straighten, lean forward and plant a soft, loving kiss between the plump, warm breasts.

When he raised his eyes to hers, they were liquid in the lamplight. "Are you ready for your dinner?" he asked. "Everything's ready."

She could only nod dumbly and wonder how his eyes could be so green and how she could, in her right mind, lie there virtually naked with his hands and lips moving over her and not even care. What had happened to all those plans to drive him out? Somewhere between her falling asleep in angry exhaustion and waking to his gentling caresses, her feelings had mellowed considerably.

"Why don't you slip this on instead of dressing again," he suggested, standing and offering a robe to her. She noticed then that all her clothes had been picked up and hung in the closet and that he had chosen her oldest, most comfortable robe for her to wear.

"J-just leave it. I'll join you in a minute."

"All right."

When he left, Laney pulled on the robe and hurried into the bathroom. She knew by his broad grin that he had understood her request. When she was done, she stared at herself in the mirror over the basin. Her hair was a tangled mess around her head, but somehow, with her rosy cheeks and sleep-laden eyes, it looked appealing and . . . seductive.

She banished that thought and ruthlessly raked a brush through her hair. Handfuls of warm water rinsed the sleep from her eyes and she rinsed her mouth out. When she felt that she was at least presentably, if not quite properly, attired to entertain a gentleman at dinner, she stepped into terry-cloth slippers and made her way through the house to the kitchen. A fire had been started in the fireplace. In spite of herself she was smiling with the pleasure of its homey glow when she entered the kitchen.

"There you are. I thought you might have fallen asleep again."

Not a chance, Laney thought ironically. After having had his warm mouth kissing the inside curves of her breasts? He must be kidding.

He had changed into comfortable clothes while she was asleep. Gone were the tailored slacks and Italian loafers, and in their place were worn jeans and scuffed jogging shoes. He had on a Harvard sweatshirt with the sleeves pushed to his elbows. An apron was tied around his waist. With a pair of tongs he was fishing spaghetti out of a boiling pot of water and transferring it to the center of a shallow serving dish.

The small table was informally but correctly set. In its center there was an opened bottle of red wine "breathing," which was something Laney was finding difficult to do. She was overwhelmed. No one had ever gone to so much trouble for her in her entire life.

"Mr. Sargent. I—"

"Oh, for Godsakes, Laney, don't start again." He finished with the spaghetti and began ladling a thick and wonderful-smelling tomato sauce over it. When it was to his liking, he faced her, hands on hips. "I can't argue on an empty stomach, and you've got two empty stomachs growling. Yours and Scooter's. And besides that, there's nothing worse—"

"Scooter's?"

"—than cold spaghetti. Now, sit down."

"Spaghetti is the last thing I need. It's fattening."

"You do need it. Sit down."

"I need fattening?" She looked down. She could barely see the tips of her toes over her stomach.

"Laney, I'm getting tired of repeating myself." He pointed an imperious finger toward the nearest chair. "Sit down, dammit."

A giggle she couldn't stop bubbled out of her mouth

and then she was laughing uncontrollably. "What are you laughing at?" he asked.

"I think I'm finding it hard to take orders from a man wearing a yellow-ruffled daisy-print apron."

He had the grace to look chagrined. "Well, the apron is coming off," he said threateningly. He untied the strings and tossed the apron onto the countertop. "And then—"

He took two steps toward her. "Oh, all right." She plopped down in the chair. The aroma of the spaghetti was making her mouth water.

"Garlic bread, hot out of the oven." He pulled the foil-wrapped bread from the oven and cursed under his breath when he burned his hand.

"I'll gain five pounds."

"You can stand it," Deke said, swinging his leg over the back of his chair and sitting down. He reached for the wine bottle and poured a small portion into Laney's glass, a more generous one into his. "Dr. Taylor said you were doing a good job keeping your weight down, but he didn't want you to starve yourself or the baby."

Laney had been spooning salad from a large bowl onto her salad plate. The oversize wooden fork and spoon halted in midair. When he finished speaking, she gradually lowered the utensils to her plate. Her hands found each other in her lap and clenched. "You spoke to Dr. Taylor?" she asked tightly. "About me?"

Deke took a sip of wine and replaced his glass on the tabletop. He looked at her for a moment, the steam from the platter of spaghetti rising between them. "Yes."

"Damn you," Laney said. All the warmth she had begun to feel after he awakened her disappeared and she was left only with that cold feeling of having been violated. "Why would he discuss a patient with a complete stranger?" She could feel tears forming in her eyes and cursed them.

"I told him what you had told everyone else: that I was your estranged husband, that you were carrying my child, and that I wanted to know how you were doing. I also admitted that I had been negligent because I didn't know about your pregnancy, but that I intended to remedy my seeming unconcern immediately."

"Dr. Taylor wouldn't have told you anything unless he checked with me first."

He made a vexed sound with his mouth. "You're too smart for your own good."

"So, where did you get all your information?" she demanded.

"From his nurse," he admitted contritely.

That Laney could believe. He could weasel the combination to the vault at Fort Knox out of a female. Her eyes narrowed with enlightenment. "You paid my bill, didn't you?"

"As any husband worth his salt would have."

"But you are *not* my husband, estranged or otherwise. I've never had a husband, nor do I want one. I manufactured an imaginary husband to keep my job. That's all. I was taking care of myself and the baby just fine without your interference. Why don't you just leave me alone?" Propping her elbows on the table, she buried her face in her hands and began to cry.

Deke came around the table, dropped to his knees and took her in his arms. "Laney, don't cry."

She tried to shove him away, but he wasn't easy to budge. "What do you expect me to do? I don't want you here. Can't you understand that? I never wanted to see you again."

"Am I such a bad choice of companion? You didn't seem to think so the night of the blackout."

"I had no choice," she said fiercely.

"You did, Laney." His voice was quiet but adamant. It compelled her to look directly into his eyes and admit the truth. She was the first to look away. "I gave you many choices. I tried not to touch you, but God, I'm only a man. And I got every indication that you were all too willing to accept my loving."

"I had had one or two drinks with Sally and Jeff. I never drink that much."

"I didn't know that. I didn't know you were a virgin."

She glared at him defensively. "I'll bet that gave you a good laugh later, didn't it? Did you share the gory details in the racquetball locker room with all the guys? What did you imagine was wrong with me?"

"Just keep this up, Laney, and you're going to make me mad as hell," he said tensely. "I thought your virginity was endearing."

"And weird, certainly unusual. Vastly different from the sophisticated women who had shared that bed with you before."

"Yes."

She felt she had been slapped in the face and she

drew in a sudden breath. Had she perversely wanted him to deny that other women had shared his bed?

"I offered to stop numerous times, Laney. You didn't want me to. Or if you did, you were saying one thing and meaning another."

"Stop," she groaned, hiding her face in her hands once more. "I don't want to remember."

"Why did you leave that morning before we could even talk?"

"I didn't want to talk. I didn't want to know you—not your name, nothing. I thought I'd never see you again. I never considered getting pregnant because I'd been told I couldn't conceive. I just wanted to walk away and forget it. I should have known better. We have to pay for our mistakes."

"You consider what happened between us a mistake?"

"Yes!" she said savagely, lifting her head to look at him. "I had a well-ordered life. I asked nothing, wanted nothing, from anyone. Now look at the mess I'm in."

"The mess and me being synonymous, I suppose."

He was smiling, actually smiling, as he squatted on his haunches beside her chair, smoothing back her hair and drying the tears from her cheeks.

"Leave me alone," she said crossly. "I can't fight you. Not physically, not verbally. I'm so tired. I want the baby, but I'm sick of being pregnant. Of looking like a blimp. Of having to go to the bathroom every ten seconds. I hate whining to you like this. Oh, God, what am I going to do?"

"Right now you're going to eat your dinner," he said practically.

He came to his feet and began heaping her plate with spaghetti. "I'm not hungry," she said petulantly.

"Yes you are. And Dr. Taylor, or rather his nurse, said that having a sip or two of wine at dinner won't hurt the baby. Hopefully it'll improve your disposition," he added under his breath, but she heard him.

"Like brandy did once?" she asked nastily.

"You didn't hear me complaining." He nuzzled her neck and let his hand slide beneath her breast for a quick caress before he returned to his own chair, "Eat. Drink."

"And be merry?"

He grinned. "That will take some work."

She was curled in a corner of the sofa, staring into the fire and sipping a cup of herbal tea, when he switched out the light in the kitchen and joined her. He sprawled on the sofa, stretching his long legs out in front of him. Without the least compunction, he took her hand between his.

"You're going to have dishpan hands," she remarked sullenly. He had insisted on clearing up the dishes after their dinner. She had been too weary and too aggravated to argue.

"Yeah. I thought most civilized people had automatic dishwashers these days."

"The house didn't come with one and I adored the house. You caught me on the maid's day off."

"You do have a housekeeper, then?"

She looked at him incredulously. "You're serious, aren't you?" She pulled her hand from between his.

With that simple question he had pointed out just how different their lives were. They might as well have come from different planets, for all they had in common. "I live on a kindergarten teacher's salary, Mr. Sargent. I live comfortably and will be able to support my child. But housekeepers are not in the budget."

"You look beautiful in the firelight, Laney."

She sighed in exasperation and let her head fall back onto the cushions. Immediately she raised it. That posture reminded her too much of the night in his apartment. The logs in the fireplace crackled and popped cheerily, mocking her melancholia. "I love having a fire on a cold night. Thank you."

He retrieved her hand. "You're welcome."

"It's been difficult for me to carry the logs inside, so—"

"I'd better not see you lifting anything heavier than a mascara wand."

When she faced him, her expression was no longer angry but pensive. "You really intend to move in here, don't you?"

"Yes."

"Why?"

He studied the shape of her fingers and nails as he spoke softly. "I want to be with you during this. Having a child is definitely an event to be shared by the parents. I want to see my child born."

She wet her lips. The strokes of his fingers against her flesh, in the palm of her hand, were eliciting strange thrills through her body. She remembered similar strokes of his tongue against her hand.

Memories of those and other caresses still alarmed her, but she didn't take her hand away. Desperately she wanted to understand why he had sought her out. She also realized the futility of denying that the child was his. What purpose would that serve? They both knew the truth.

"Even if I agreed, how could you stay here until the baby was born? You have a busy life in New York— your law practice."

"A staff of assistants is taking care of it. I'll give you the details if you like, but—"

"No." She was shaking her head. There were other things she wanted to know, things she couldn't help being curious about. "You must have family, friends, who want to know why you left everything to come to Arkansas of all places. Surely you didn't tell them about me?"

"My family is quite large," he said, smiling fondly. "When the time is right, you'll meet them." Laney paled at the thought of a multitude of snobby New Yorkers assessing her with distaste. "But in the meantime I told them I was taking some time off for personal business. They were curious, but they respect my privacy." He kissed the back of her palm and ran his hand caressingly up her arm, slipping it into the wide sleeve of her robe.

"As to the other, I have very few friends I deem worthy of confidences about you."

"And other . . . uh . . ."

"Women?" She shrugged noncommittally. "I've never been married. I've been semiseriously involved with a few and casually involved with many."

"I see," she said, swallowing hard, wishing for more information on that aspect of his life and at the same time glad she didn't know.

"What about your family?" he asked.

"I have none."

"None?"

"No. No one."

"And no young men to explain me to?"

Lying was useless. "No."

"I haven't been to bed with a woman since we were together."

She was stunned, and the face she turned on him told him so. "I don't believe you," she whispered. A man like him, suave, apparently wealthy and virile. She could testify to his potency.

"Oh, you'll believe me soon enough. My temper is mighty testy these days." He was laughing softly, but his expression changed swiftly. "Laney, I want you. And I want my baby. I'm too old to play games, and I don't want to mess this up any more than I already did the morning you woke up with me. This means too much to me to foul up."

He stood and went to the fireplace. With a poker he idly stirred the coals beneath the logs until the flames leaped high again. "I could have come on to you gradually, wooed you, courted you. But I probably would have made a damn fool of myself. Not to mention the embarrassment it would have caused you." He turned to her and treated her to a glimpse of straight white teeth as he smiled. "Most people, especially in this part of the country, wouldn't have considered a pregnant lady estranged from her husband courtable. Besides, patience has never been one of my virtues. I like to see results quickly." He walked toward her. "I can tell by your expression that you're still bothered by my being here. Do I repel you? Does the thought of having made love with me repel you?"

She answered honestly. "No."

He hid a quick smile of relief. "Ah, well, that's good. Is it my age? How old are you?"

"Twenty-seven."

"I'm relieved. I thought you were younger. There's sixteen years difference in our ages. Does that bother you?"

"No, Deke." And when she heard his name on her lips, she yanked her head upright to see if he had noticed. He had. He settled beside her on the couch.

"Then what is it, Laney?"

"It's everything," she said, spreading her arms wide. "You. Me. Our ages are the least of our differences. We don't even know each other, except . . ." She shook off the persistent memory of their night together. Ah, Laney, you're sweet, he thought.

"I know every inch of you." He slipped his hand into her robe and encircled her throat, massaging the triangle at its base with a hypnotic thumb. "You know me too. We touched everywhere, explored each other, kissed everything."

Spots of scarlet flared in her cheeks. "We don't know each other in the ways that count."

He folded her into his arms and pressed her head to his chest. "That's why I'm here. I want us to get to know each other before we're introduced to this other little person." He laid his hand on the bulging curve of her stomach just under her breasts. "And that's the first thing I want to know."

She was puzzled. "What?"

"Why you, Laney McLeod, a beautiful young woman, warm and caring as you are, shrink defensively every time I touch you."

Alarm sirens shrieked in her head. He was getting too close. Not physically. He couldn't get any closer physically than they had already been. But he was getting too close to her fears, her inner self. "I don't."

"You do. Each time I touch you, you tense up. I can *feel* a hesitation, almost a fear, inside you, Laney. Only when your students touch you do you let that invisible guard down. What are you afraid of, Laney? Why do you flinch when you're caressed?"

She swallowed hard. Her voice was thready and she tried to inject anger into it, but didn't think she was successful. "Can you blame me? I'm hardly accustomed to a strange man moving in on me, touching and fondling me. Turn the tables and ask yourself what you would do, how you would feel."

He cupped her face in his hands and stared down into her eyes for what seemed to her an uncomfortable eternity. "There's more to it than that. The night you were in my apartment, you were starved for the touch of another human being—you were craving love. You're a sad lady, Laney McLeod, and I intend to find out why. All a part of making you merry."

He kissed her lightly. "Just for the record, if you

moved in on me and wanted to touch me, I'd be wild with happiness." Once more his lips swept hers. "Go to bed now. You've had a hard day."

He pulled her to her feet as he rose and gave her a gentle push toward the bedroom. She went without an argument. She picked out something to wear to school the next day and prepared for bed. She was just about to pull the covers back when Deke walked in.

"I'm going to wait until morning to unpack," he commented, yawning. "We're low on milk. Do you have it delivered or do you buy it at the grocery store?"

"I buy it. What are you doing?" she asked breathlessly as he peeled off his sweatshirt.

"I'm taking off my shirt." He tossed the shirt aside and sat down on the bed, pulled off his shoes and let them drop. "Now I'm taking off my pants." He stood, unsnapped and unzipped the bleached and frayed jeans and let them fall. He stepped out of them, bent down, scooped them up and began to fold them. He laid them neatly in a chair and turned to face her, totally unabashed that he was wearing only a pair of tight white briefs. "Aren't you cold? Get in under the covers."

She stood transfixed and watched him walk around the bed to where she was standing with one hand on the bedspread and the other over her pounding heart.

"You look like a rich, creamy dessert," he said, clasping her by the shoulders and letting his green eyes feast on her appreciatively.

The yellow nightgown was old, but she liked it and it was comfortable. It was sleeveless and had a scooped neckline that showed quite a bit of cleavage, now that her breasts were larger. A ribbon was tied under the bosom to form an empire style. The floor-length skirt was full and loose enough to accommodate her stomach. It had never occurred to her how sheer it was until this moment and she was alarmingly aware of her nakedness beneath it. Mainly because Deke was inspecting her so intimately.

"Your nipples have changed color too. They're darker, aren't they? I like the change." His hand touched first one sensitive tip, then the other. There may as well have been no nightgown, for his fingertips branded her flesh. "Come on. In with you."

Deke pushed her toward the bed, but she resisted like an inflatable toy that is weighted at the bottom and can't be knocked over. Barely finding her voice after his familiar caress, she gasped, "You can't be planning to sleep in here with me?"

"I'm planning on that, yes."

"You can't!"

"Why?"

"*Why!* Because I don't want you to, that's why. You can stay the night, since it's late. But in the morning you have to leave. I'll figure out some solution to our . . . uh . . ."

"Problem?"

"Yes, problem," she shouted back, infuriated by his calm.

He turned away from her, took several pacing steps while he studied the floor, then spun back around, asking brusquely, "Where do you propose that I sleep?" She could all but see him in the courtroom, demanding of some poor soul, "Where were you on the night of the murder?" His eyes bored into her. His stance was intimidating, even if his costume wasn't exactly the three-piece suit he probably wore to court. "There's no bed in the other bedroom, and I'll be damned before I'll contort my seventy-five inches to fit a sixty-inch sofa."

"You should have thought of that before you barged—Oh!" she exclaimed, grasping her side.

"What is it? God. Oh, hell. Laney? What's the matter?"

"Nothing, nothing," she said, from her bent position. Slowly she straightened, impatiently warding off his examining hands. "Just a cramp," she said between shallow pants. "It happens sometimes."

"Have you told the doctor? What did he say? Is it gone now? How often does this happen? God, don't ever scare me like that."

They were both bundled into the bed by now, swathed by covers, and his hands were moving over her as though searching for possible injuries.

"It's gone now. I'm all right."

"You're sure?"

"Yes. Deke—"

"I like to hear you say my name."

"Deke, stop—"

She was never allowed to finish. His mouth got in the way. "Just a kiss, Laney. Just a kiss." He sipped at her lips to keep them silent, teasing and playing until he tired of games. His tongue became a master that gentled even as it tamed. He stroked her tongue into enthusiastic participation, and she felt her resistance slipping as her mouth melded with his. They drank of each other thirstily.

He engulfed her. His scent, his taste, the feel of his hair-rough skin against hers, became as essential as they had once before. That need deep within her resurrected itself. If she didn't have his touch, if he didn't kiss her, she would surely die. His manhood was hot and hard against her thigh. She wanted to know it again inside her, deep and full and pulsing, filling the void that was her life. But she couldn't let him know. She couldn't.

"Laney," he murmured as he dragged his mouth from hers. He licked her lips with the tip of his tongue. "You are delicious. Better than any dessert. No matter how much of you I had, I would never get my fill." His lips moved across her face to the side of her neck, where he took tiny love bites. "God, I've dreamed of this for months. I've missed you since the moment I realized you were gone. I've been longing to hold you again, to feel your sweet body against mine, to taste you."

His hand found her breasts, warm and full. Gently he massaged them, running his palms over them lightly until the nipples responded. He dipped his head and kissed them through the gauzy fabric of her nightgown, wetting the cloth as his tongue nudged the peaks. Laney made a small crying sound that echoed his. His head came up immediately.

"Damn," he sighed self-reproachfully. He laid his head against her breasts until his breathing slowed and his passion subsided.

When at last he lifted himself and looked at her, his

eyes were sparking with an internal fire that had been temporarily banked but not quenched. It still smoldered. "I've bullied you all day. I won't rush you into this too. When I joined you in here tonight, I promised myself that we were going to sleep and nothing else." He reached over and turned out the light. "How do you usually sleep?"

Laney's whole body was flushed with desire. She had to concentrate on keeping her breathing steady. She couldn't let him know that beneath the surface her heart was racing. She knew all she had to do was touch him, lay a hand on him in wordless entreaty, and he would throw his conscience aside and make love to her. But much as she wanted that, she couldn't let it happen. Better to let him call things off than to regret impulsive behavior later. She rolled onto her side to face the outside. "Like this."

"Good. I won't bump you in the night. Good night." He lifted her hair from the back of her neck and planted a soft kiss there. His feet found hers to warm them. He laid his arm along hers and cupped her shoulder with his hand.

Laney couldn't believe she was allowing this. Passion was one thing; it required nothing of the emotions. Anyone could experience it. But sleeping with someone, actually sleeping, was as good as a commitment. Emotional commitments meant taking risks she couldn't afford. Making even a minor commitment to this man was unthinkable. More than anyone, he had the power to hurt her. He was still a stranger. But Lord, how familiar a stranger he was.

She enjoyed the feel of his breath on her neck. The warmth emanating from him permeated her whole body. The night wasn't so dark and lonely with him beside her. There was someone to absorb the night noises and make them less frightening. One more night with him couldn't hurt.

She slept with a clear conscience.

CHAPTER | 5

In the morning, however, she had to justify her actions. The rationalizations she had made the evening before didn't sound so convincing in the light of day. As she rushed through showering and applying her makeup, she was once again dismayed by her behavior. Why had she allowed him to sleep with her, to hold her through the night?

Once, when the baby had become rambunctious, she had stirred restlessly, willing it to relax and let her get her much needed rest.

Deke's arm had tightened around her and he had whispered in her ear, "Everything all right?"

"I have to go to the bathroom." She struggled free of his embrace and the covers, rushed to the bathroom and then came back, eager for the warmth of the bed. Not a little of that warmth came from Deke.

When she was once again wrapped in his arms and

lying against his hard body he murmured, "Scooter acting up?"

"Yes," she sighed and shifted to another position, seeking a comfortable one.

Deke's hand came around her, settled on her stomach and soothingly rubbed it. Apparently the baby was entranced as much as Laney, for in moments the fetal movements stopped and Laney was permitted to drift back to sleep.

Now, giving herself one final inspection before leaving the bedroom, she admitted how good it was having someone to share both the joy and the discomfort with.

Deke hadn't been in the bed when her alarm went off, and as she made her way through the house she heard him clattering in the kitchen. "What is all this?" she asked as she entered the sunny room.

He was buttering a stack of toast. "Whatever happened to 'Good morning'?" He came to kiss her quickly on the cheek. "In answer to your question, this is breakfast."

"I don't eat breakfast. Maybe toast and coffee."

"Not enough for you and Scooter." He pointed toward the chair. "You'd better get started or the school bell will ring without you."

She looked at the plate on the table and groaned. Scrambled eggs, bacon, two slices of toast, grapefruit juice and coffee. "I can't eat all this." His granite expression told her that arguing was futile. Last night he had made her eat what seemed like tubs of spaghetti.

He wouldn't listen to her protests now either. Resignedly she placed her purse and book bag on one of the empty chairs and sat down to eat.

When she had packed down enough to satisfy him, he went out to start her car so she wouldn't have to cope with the troublesome engine and so the interior would be warm for her. At the front door he held her coat and buttoned her into it. She apologized for leaving him with dirty dishes again.

He brushed her apologies aside. "Put on your gloves. It's cold this morning. I'm going to have to do something about that car of yours. It's cranky as hell."

His breath froze in the morning air and the new sun glinted on his silver hair. She found herself actually basking in the careful attention he paid her. But this couldn't last, and the sooner he was out of her life, the better. "Deke, we must talk."

"We are talking."

"I mean it. I'm serious."

"So am I. Drive carefully."

"You're talking but you're not listening! Promise me you won't unpack your things. Promise me."

"I promise." He kissed her with rushed ardor. "Now, scoot. I don't want you to drive fast to keep from being late."

She went, but she wasn't convinced of his compliance. He had agreed too easily. He looked too well ensconced, too much at home standing on her front porch as he waved her off, too self-assured and content. No, he wasn't going to leave without a fight.

The day was hectic. The teachers didn't even attempt to teach. The children were wound up like chatterboxes with Christmas holiday excitement. Laney's class decorated coffee mugs to give to their moms. The depictions were innovative to say the least, but Laney knew the mothers would treasure them.

Helping each child wrap his gift in colored paper, she got all teary-eyed as she thought of one day receiving a gift from her own child. She would hug him and exclaim over the worth of his present. He would know how much she appreciated his efforts to make something for her.

In all her daydreams the child had green eyes that were both intelligent and filled with humor. Impatient with her musings, she shoved the images aside.

Today, as soon as she got home, she would demand that Deke leave. What he proposed to do was impossible. He couldn't stay with her, pretending to be married to her. After the baby came, then what? If he was this possessive with her, how would he be with his child?

The thought made Laney's blood run cold. He wouldn't try to take the baby away from her, would he? No! She wouldn't let that happen if she had to flee the country and change her identity. Nothing was going to separate her from her child. Not even a force as powerful and influential as Deke Sargent, Attorney at Law.

What then could she do?

Bargain? Yes, they would bargain like civilized

adults. She would tell him that he could see the child frequently, whenever it was convenient for her. She wouldn't prevent her child from knowing his father. They would be like a divorced couple: Deke would be a father with visiting privileges.

It wasn't the ideal solution, but it was the best she could come up with both to satisfy him and to get him out of her life as quickly as he had entered it.

After the Christmas turkey lunch, while the children were resting before their party, Laney sat at her desk and made notes. She would appear more businesslike and less emotional if she presented him with a tentative agreement on when and where and for how long he could see the child each year. Of course, for the first year or so, it couldn't be very often. As the child grew older the visiting time would increase. It tore at Laney's heart to think of her child going away to stay all summer with Deke. He would lavish the child with presents, take him places that would be financially beyond her. What if the child came to love him more than he did her?

That wouldn't happen. She would see to it.

Her hands gripped the wheel of her car nervously as she drove home. School had been dismissed an hour early, due to the holiday, but this was one day she didn't look forward to arriving home. She had a plan all worked out on paper. But suggesting it to Deke and getting him to agree to it was an ordeal she dreaded. With his talent for turning a phrase, he could tear her document to shreds.

Her nervousness changed to curiosity as she turned onto her block and saw that several vehicles were parked in her driveway. An old Ford, a new Mercedes station wagon, numerous trucks. What was going on? As a million possibilities assailed her, fury overtook her.

Damn him! No telling what he was up to. She had been a fool to leave him alone in her house. She braked the car and slammed the door behind her as she stalked to the front door and pushed it open.

The house was in utter chaos. A hefty woman in a full apron and orthopedic shoes was wielding the vacuum cleaner around the living-room floor. She looked pointedly at the stranger sitting quietly on the sofa, holding his briefcase on his lap. Obediently he raised his feet and let her sweep beneath them. Another man was kneeling in front of the baseboard, tapping down a telephone cord. There was pounding and hammering coming from the kitchen. Laney could hear Deke's voice over the raucous noise, shouting, "Don't bang into the walls, please. Can't you see that Laney recently painted them? Careful, man."

The telephone rang, and before Laney could answer it, the woman with the vacuum cleaner grabbed it up. "No, he's busy at the moment, but if you'll hold on, I'll call him." She put the phone aside and turned to see Laney, her mouth slack with astonishment, still standing in the door.

"Why, hello, Ms. McLeod. I'm Mrs. Thomas. I've seen you at the school. My little girl, Teresa, is in fifth grade. You might shut the door. Cold air is getting in. I've got to fetch Mr. Sargent to the phone."

Laney stood dumbly as the smiling woman bustled toward the bedrooms, calling, "Mr. Sargent, telephone again."

" 'Scuse me."

Laney whipped around to see a brash young man in tight jeans, a denim jacket and a battered cowboy hat leaning against the doorjamb. "This the place where I was s'pposed to deliver a dishwasher today or else forget it?" He smiled, popped his chewing gum and winked at her all at the same time.

"Dammit, I said not to bang the walls," Deke roared from the back of the house. "Yes, Mrs. Thomas, thank you. Tell them I'm coming."

"Excuse me, ma'am," someone said softly from behind Laney. A heavyset man was trying to make his way around her through the door. He had on a carpenter's belt from which several tools dangled on his hips. "I need more nails from my truck." Like an automaton, she moved aside and let him pass.

"He's coming, but you'll have to hang on a moment," Mrs. Thomas said into the phone.

"I need to speak to him too," the man on the couch said timidly.

"He knows that. He'll be with you soon." The vacuum was started again.

"Laney!" was Deke's happy exclamation when he came bounding through the door with the agility of a NFL halfback. "What are you doing home so early?

Oh, damn"—he slapped his forehead with the heel of his hand—"I forgot you dismissed early today. I wanted all this done before you got here."

"What the hell is going on?" Laney shouted. She faced Deke, her body rigid, her face red and her eyes flashing with anger.

The man in the cowboy hat whistled softly through his teeth. The carpenter, who had returned with the nails, coughed self-consciously behind his hand. Mrs. Thomas turned off the vacuum, which whined to a deadly silence. She quietly told the person on the telephone to call back and hung it up. Two men Laney had never seen before crowded into the door leading to the bedroom hallway and stood gaping at her. The hammering in the kitchen ceased and another stranger filled that doorway. The man on the sofa stood, thought better of it and sat back down. The telephone installer came up off the floor. They all looked at her curiously, as though she were the one out of place and possibly out of her mind.

Heaving in a great breath and trying to hang on to her slipping sanity, she asked in a softer, if faltering, voice, "What is going on, Deke? Who are all these people and what are they doing in my house?"

He took her purse and book bag and helped her off with her coat as he said calmly, "That is Mrs. Thomas, whose purpose I think is self-explanatory. She's been hired to clean, since I'm no good at it and hate it and since you shouldn't be doing it. Also to cook, because I can prepare exactly two menus, spaghetti and scrambled eggs, and you've had those already." He turned to the housekeeper and smiled. "She's already put a pot roast in the oven."

The man on the sofa caught Deke's attention by waving a tentative finger at him. "Oh, Mr. Smalley. I'd almost forgotten you." Deke turned to Laney. "He delivered your new car, but I haven't had a chance to sign all the papers yet." To the man he said, "I'll be right with you."

"Phone's ready," said the installer, and he began to gather up his tools.

"He put in a new WATS line so I can conduct business from here and stay in touch with my office," Deke explained. He pointed to the two men in the doorway. "They are dismantling the old bed and assembling the new one and taxing my patience by scarring the walls." Shamefacedly they shuffled back toward the largest bedroom and disappeared.

"New car? New bed! I don't need a new bed."

"Perhaps *you* don't. But *we* do."

The young man in the cowboy hat said "Hot damn" under his breath and crossed his arms over his chest, looking for all the world like he was enjoying the show.

"Excuse me. I'll just squeeze through here. . . ." The carpenter edged past Laney again, apologetically mumbling something about finishing and getting out of their way as soon as possible.

"He and his helper are taking out a cabinet in the kitchen to make room for the dishwasher and this . . ." His voice dwindled as he glared at the young man, who was eyeing Laney in a way that made Deke's eyes go hard and cold. "Who are you?"

"I'm the dishwasher," the young man replied jauntily.

"I think the carpenters are ready for you. You'll get the machine in easier through the back door."

"Right." He let his eyes travel from the top of Laney's head to the tip of her boots, stopping significantly on her pregnant stomach. He cocked a knowing eyebrow at Deke and, popping his gum loudly and tipping his hat, said, "Way to go, buddy."

"You promised," Laney said accusingly as she sat down on the couch, totally spent.

"I promised not to unpack and I haven't." Deke seated himself beside her on the sofa and patted his thighs. "Put your feet up here."

Because she was too tired to argue and wanted to relieve the swelling in her feet and ankles anyway, she leaned back and raised her feet to his lap. He unzipped her boots and pulled them off and began to massage her feet with adept fingers.

The house had been cleared of people. Somehow Deke had effected that in an amazingly short period of time while she watched, feeling utterly useless.

"I'll build another fire tonight and you can toast your toes on the hearth. Your feet are freezing again. Just like they were last night in bed. But we warmed them up, didn't we?" He dragged a seductive finger down her high arch.

"Don't change the subject," she said, trying to extricate her foot from his hands and failing to. "Deke, you practically redesigned my house today."

"I bought you a new bed with a firm mattress guaranteed for ten years and had a new dishwasher with every conceivable option installed. It has a three-year service contract. Tell me what's wrong with all that."

"What will the landlady say?"

"That the dishwasher stays when you move. Otherwise she was delighted with the improvement."

"And the car and Mrs. Thomas?"

"Consider the car one of your Christmas presents. And I hired Mrs. Thomas as much for me as for you."

"But that's just it," she said, snatching her feet from his hands and sitting upright. "You won't be here that long." She stood up and crossed to the window, folding her arms beneath her bosom and hugging her elbows with her hands. It had become necessary to put as much space between them as possible. When she was close to him she relaxed, and when she relaxed . . .

"You have to leave. Today." When he didn't respond but remained silent behind her, she continued. "I truly appreciate your concern for me. I certainly didn't expect it from you in this era of sexual freedom. I didn't expect you to care what happened to either me or the child. I accept full responsibility for that night in New York, including the responsibility of rearing my child alone."

"That's unfair of you, Laney. He's my child too. Despite my marital status, I have a great respect for family, tradition, having an heir, that type of old-fashioned thing. Sexual freedom and responsibilities be damned. None of that has anything to do with why I'm here."

A deep breath did little to relieve her qualms about the subject she must broach. "I've thought about your relationship to the baby. Quite a lot, as a matter of fact. It would be unfair to keep the child from knowing you and . . . and you from knowing him. So I'm willing to let you visit often. When the child is older and can leave home, he can come see you." The words cost her dearly and she almost choked on them. Clearing her throat loudly, she went to her purse and took out the document she had deliberated over.

"I wrote down what I think will be a fair arrangement. Look it over and let me know what you think. I'll be happy to discuss it with you." She extended the paper to him, then returned to her place at the window and waited tensely.

After five long minutes of silence she heard the sound of tearing paper and turned to see him neatly ripping the document she had so painstakingly written out. "Oh," she cried out in anger. "That was a fair proposal for all of us, Deke. For the child too."

"You miss the point, Laney." Getting up, he came toward her with what looked like a predator's determination. He slid one arm around her waist and hauled her close. At the same time he tangled the fingers of his other hand in the hair at her nape and brought her face close to his. "The point was not to badger you into giving me visiting rights. And it wasn't to threaten you with taking the child away from you. Dammit! What kind of a monster do you take me for? What have I ever done to make you think you would have to protect yourself, your child—*my* child—from me?"

"You took advantage of a weakness once before."

"Perhaps I did," he confessed roughly.

"I'll never let you do it again."

His mouth was a grim, hard line, but his eyes were fiery. "I don't want to take advantage of you. I want you in my life. Did you think I could just let you disappear after that night, Laney? Didn't you know I would seek you out, leave no stone unturned until I found you? Long before I knew about the baby, I was determined to find you and make you mine permanently."

"But—"

"Shut up and listen to me," he said sternly, and brought her mouth closer to his so that she could feel each word as a puff of breath against her lips before it fell on her ears. "Didn't you know you were different? Didn't you know that after all the women I've been with—and I'm not bragging or trying to impress you, but merely stating a fact I'm not too proud of—I would see that difference—*feel* it? I did and I couldn't forget it. What happened between us that night was right, Laney. So right that I knew I had never had that kind of experience before. And from it came a child. Our child."

"It was an accident." She struggled against the turmoil of her emotions. One part of her reveled in what he was saying and wanted to savor every word. The other told her not to listen, to be wary, to remain inviolate. "We were caught up in unusual circumstances that could never be matched."

"We're not caught up in anything now. There's no blackout, no claustrophobia, no hysteria, no brandy. It's the middle of the afternoon and the sun is shining. If it was all an accident, why do I want you now more than ever?"

He positioned himself so that she couldn't ignore the strength of his desire. His masculinity pressed hard against her and every erogenous part of her body responded to its message.

"You want me because of the baby. That's all," she said.

His mouth was a magical tormentor that left burning kisses over her lips and cheeks and chin. "This has nothing to do with the baby," he growled and rubbed himself against her. "Now, stop all this foolishness and kiss me."

Uttering one last ragged moan, she let her mouth be fused to his with a searing heat. His lips twisted over hers as his tongue plowed between her teeth. His kiss created a heat that spilled into her veins and spread through her body like honey, melting the most steadfast of her inhibitions and objections. She fell victim again to that debilitating weakness, a delicious lassitude, that only his embraces elicited.

A wanton sound purred out of her throat as her arms

instinctively went around him. He sighed into her mouth. "Yes, Laney. Don't hold back. Trust me. Come to me as you did that night."

His kiss was gentle on her swollen lips. His mouth whispered devilishly until she was whipped into a frenzy of need. When she anxiously called his name, he made love to her mouth with a bold tongue.

"Oh, Lord," she sighed minutes later as his tongue bathed her upper lip with the dew of their kiss. "Why do you do this to me?"

He chose to misunderstand. "Because you're gorgeous and young and fresh. Because you're beautiful to look at and delightful to touch and luscious to taste. Because once you held me deep inside you and now my baby is there."

"That's not what I meant."

"I know. But those are facts just the same." His lips brushed her ear as he whispered. Even his breath against her flesh was a caress. Her head was thrown back in shameless abandon.

Her dress was hunter green with a cream-colored collar. It buttoned down the front with pearl buttons and hung straight with only a slight A-line flair to flatter her maternal figure. During that breathy conversation his hands had worked several of the buttons free.

But when he slid his hand inside and fondled her nylon-covered breast, the delirium of the moment shattered and Laney went rigid in his arms. "No," she protested fearfully, though she didn't try to escape his embrace.

His words were gently persuading. "Laney, there's nothing wrong with lovers caressing each other."

"We're not lovers."

"Yes we are. You're carrying my child. I've touched you much more intimately than this." He kissed her mouth softly. "I want to touch you, to put my hand against your sweet breast."

"You can't," she protested weakly. His hand felt so good and warm as his fingers curved around the full globe.

"I already did. Last night. I kissed you. Here." His thumb lightly teased the nipple and it hardened responsively. "Touched you with my tongue." She stifled a groan against his shirtfront, which was warm and vibrant and smelled of him. She could feel the texture of the hair covering his skin. "All I'm asking now is to touch you. Last night it was dark and we were under covers. I want to touch you in the daylight, to see my hands on you. To see yours on me."

He was nuzzling her neck with his nose and mouth, flicking her ear with his tongue. But the caresses weren't frightening. Indeed, they seemed to alleviate her fears.

Her whole body awakened to new sensations, sensations she had felt but once before. Vague and nebulous then, they now rushed to the forefront of her mind, and she selfishly, almost frantically, wanted to experience them again before they vanished. Her breasts felt full and heavy, and it wasn't from pregnancy. Her nipples strained against her brassiere and tingled with longing, begging his fingers not to desert them.

When Deke's lips maneuvered hers apart and the tip of his tongue darted into her mouth, the last vestiges of hesitation fell away. Tension ebbed out of her and her whole body flowed against his. He felt the change immediately and he rumbled approval.

"Sweetheart, you never have to fear me. Never."

At that moment she didn't think so either. Her hands slipped inside his shirt collar and went behind his neck. She bowed her body against his, harboring his male hardness in the soft hollow of her femininity. What happened to her each time she was with him, why she responded to this man and no other, she couldn't say. She didn't have an answer and didn't want to search for one as his mouth mated with hers and his hand slipped inside the cup of her brassiere to reward her flesh with the feel of his palm and fingertips against it.

Then gradually he withdrew. His hand settled over her breast in loving possession before he replaced the lacy bra and lifted his mouth from hers. As he peered into her eyes he rebuttoned her dress. Her eyes were eloquent with an unspoken question.

"This is a learning process," he answered quietly, grazing her lips softly with his. "I'm teaching you to trust me, taking one step at a time." He sucked in a deep breath. "And both I and the zipper on my pants have undergone just about as much stress as we can in the course of this lesson."

She blushed furiously and ducked her head. He laughed and hugged her tight, rocking back and forth. "You're adorable. Here you are, almost seven months pregnant, and your modesty would make one think you'd never been with a man."

"I barely remember it."

He pushed her away from him and forced her to meet his eyes. His finger outlined the shape of her bottom lip, which was still throbbing and full from their recent kisses. "You remember," he slurred.

Then, with an abrupt change of mood, he pointed her in the direction of the bedroom, swatted her bottom and said, "Go change into something comfortable while I dish up the pot roast."

The light mood lasted through the excellent dinner Mrs. Thomas had left in the oven for them. After the dishes were done, they went out and bought a Christmas tree off the Optimist club lot. Laney declared that it was too large for the house and Deke dubbed her a Scrooge, a name that seemed even more fitting when he learned she didn't have any decorations. He practically bought out the variety store's stock of lights, balls and tinsel.

The next several days were like none other in Laney's life. Deke insisted that he bring her breakfast in bed every morning. He pampered her to the point of being ridiculous. Over her protests he instructed her on the use of all the gadgets in the new station wagon.

"Why should I learn to drive this mechanical Disneyland? You're taking it back when you return to New York."

"No one keeps a car in Manhattan."

"What about that one?" She pointed a finger at the Cadillac.

"I leased that in Tulsa while I was running all over the city, looking for you."

That shut her up and she conceded to drive the new car. Besides, her old one had mysteriously disappeared, and dynamite wouldn't blast its whereabouts out of Deke.

They shopped for things for the baby and bought a new bedspread for the king-size bed. Meticulous to the last detail, Deke had ordered linens and blankets, which had been delivered along with it.

"It was so nice of you to leave choosing the bed-spread to me," Laney said sarcastically.

He swooped down on her mouth and met it with a resounding kiss that caused other shoppers to stop and stare. "I love your mouth when it pouts like that."

Self-conscious about the amused attention they were attracting, she muttered out of the side of her mouth, "Remind me not to pout again."

"I'll only find some other reason to kiss you."

Whenever they were out, he treated her like a piece of rare porcelain that might break at any moment. His arm was always around her, his hand under her elbow. He besieged her with questions about her well-being.

"Are you getting tired? . . . Is your back beginning to ache? . . . Are your ankles swelling again? I intend to ask Dr. Taylor about that."

She had given up demanding that he leave. She couldn't even justify her decision to let him stay. All she knew was that her cozy house was cozier now with his masculine clutter about. She liked the scent of his cologne lingering in the bathroom and on the bed linens. She even liked his salty, tangy smell when he came in from jogging or playing racquetball. It was foreign to her, this blatant maleness, but she found that she had no aversion to it. She liked the noise he made when he was dressing in the bedroom, as well as the silences they shared while they watched television or read side by side in front of the fire.

The days passed with a kind of lazy peacefulness that was new to her. He didn't pursue a sexual relationship and she was too confused to define her feelings about that. He rarely touched her but for an affectionate kiss or gesture of courtesy. Each night in the wide bed he held her against him and commiserated when the baby wouldn't let her sleep, but he didn't initiate lovemaking. She had grown used to his hard body beside her, his comforting arms around her, the sound of his gentle breathing in cadence with hers.

Necessity made for more familiarity.

In an emergency she tapped on the bathroom door one morning. When he pulled it open, he was standing with only a towel wrapped around his middle. Water was still beaded like diamonds on the luxuriant hair on his chest. His gray hair had been dried with only a towel and clung damply to his head.

"What is it? Never mind," he said, holding up both

hands, palms turned out. "I know." He quickly vacated the bathroom for her.

When she came out, his back was to her as he stood in front of the bureau. He was pulling a pair of briefs up his legs. For a moment she was held spellbound by the male perfection of his body. She watched the play of muscles in his thighs and buttocks as he slipped the stretchy cotton over them. She gasped softly, but later she swore to herself that she hadn't.

Hearing her, he turned around. "All done? May I have the bathroom back?" She nodded vigorously and all but raced from the room, her palms wet and her heart pounding.

She would let him stay. The decision really wasn't hers to make, but she passed down the judgment that he could stay with her . . . only until the baby was born. She would stand firm on that. Once the child was born, he would return to New York and she would go on with her life. They would work out an arrangement to share the child.

He could stay if he behaved himself. But she refused to grow fond of or dependent on him.

"Remind me to give Mrs. Thomas a raise. I've never eaten better stuffing."

"Around here it's called dressing and the secret is in the amount of sage one adds," Laney said.

It was Christmas day and they were replete as they sat at the dining-room table. The housekeeper had come the day before and prepared everything so that all they had to do was put the meal in the oven and set the specified time on the oven timer.

"Well, if you're so smart, maybe I'll save her salary and let you take over the cooking."

"You should do that anyway," Laney said, standing up. She began scraping the plates and stacking them on a tray.

Deke laughed. "No I shouldn't, especially when you begin the next semester. I don't suppose I can talk you into not going back."

Laney's hands froze and she stared at him, horrified. "Of course not!"

He shook his head in disgust "That's what I was afraid of."

"Whether you think so or not, my work is important."

"I—"

"I have a master's degree I worked hard to get. I care about the children. Kindergarten is probably the most critical—"

"Laney, I'm not arguing," he said quietly.

She swallowed the next segment of her tirade and said on a more reasonable note, "I like my work very much, Deke. It's important to me. Until—" She had started to say ". . . until you . . ." but amended it. "—until the baby, that's all I had. I'm a good teacher and want to continue teaching always."

"I was half teasing when I suggested that you sit out the semester, Laney. I was only thinking that it might be easier on you if you did."

She shook her head. "It would only make the time pass more slowly."

He began helping with the chore of clearing the table. "When do you go back?"

"The day after New Year's."

"And when is your next vacation?"

"March. I plan to have the baby during the spring break."

"No holiday until then?"

His questions were a little too casual, a little too subtle, a little too much like a shrewd attorney's preliminary probing before the thundering interrogation. Immediately she became suspicious. Setting a wineglass carefully on the tray, she looked at him steadily. "Why? Why are you asking about holidays?"

He shrugged nonchalantly. "I was trying to decide when we should get married."

CHAPTER | 6

Deke had expected a reaction. He got more of one than he'd bargained for. At his mention of matrimony Laney paled visibly and the tray of dishes almost slipped from her shaking hands. Her eyes rounded with disbelief and something akin to fear. Her breasts heaved beneath the soft tunic she was wearing over maternity slacks.

"I will never get married." She swallowed hard. "You've gotten your way about everything else, Mr. Sargent, but understand this: I will never marry you. I'll never marry anybody." She whirled away from him and went into the kitchen.

Deke was stymied for only a moment. His impulse was to charge after her and demand why she was so opposed to marriage. But taking into account the determination that had made the bones of her face stand out prominently, he realized that browbeating would be the wrong tack. She had adamantly refused. Pressing her for an explanation would only make her retreat into that invisible, but nonetheless real, corner where she often hid. For the past several days he had coaxed her out of that shell, and he didn't want to do anything that might undermine the confidence he had won.

He entered the kitchen behind her. She was rinsing dishes and placing them in the new dishwasher. "I've heard of women's liberation, but I didn't know it precluded marriage."

"I'm not a women's libber. I just never want to marry."

She wouldn't look at him and that was irritating. He wanted to jerk her around and insist that she look at him. But her body was strained as tight as a piano wire. He wanted to see her relaxed and smiling again. Something haunted her. If it was the last thing he did, he intended to find out what that something was and exorcise it.

"I thought most young girls grew up dreaming about a husband and children."

"I'm hardly a young girl. And I told you I thought I couldn't have children."

"I assumed you were just saying that."

She turned around then, and inside he gloated. He had nettled her, provoked her to anger, but he had succeeded in getting her to face him.

"It's the truth. I was told when I was thirteen that I would be barren because of a secondary infection resulting from appendicitis."

"So that's when you made up your mind never to marry."

She shook her head. "No."

"When?"

"I always knew I would never have . . . I didn't want . . ."

"A man in your life?"

"Yes."

"Any man?"

"Yes."

"You could have fooled me. Especially that night in New York."

Her jaw clamped tightly shut. "Don't be disgusting." She faced the sink again and began to scrub a cooking pan ruthlessly.

"I'm not trying to be disgusting," he began with a level voice. "I'm trying to be practical. I'm trying to find out why a beautiful young woman about to have a baby won't even consider marrying the father of said baby when he could make life so much easier, and I think happier, for her and her child. And dammit, please look at me while I'm talking to you," he finished in a shout.

He berated himself for letting his temper get the better of him, but when she turned icy eyes on him and faced him with a belligerent set to her jaw, his contrition dissolved. If she wanted a fight, a fight she would get. It was a foregone conclusion she would lose. His eyes treated her to the same truth-seeking stare he gave to a witness he knew was lying.

"You're not frigid." His voice lowered to a silky tone. "We both know that."

"I'm glad you told me you weren't trying to be disgusting. Otherwise I might think you were."

"You like my touch, you like my lovemaking, I think you even like me. So what's the problem, Laney? Why did you panic when I mentioned marriage?"

"You want to be practical? Okay, we'll be practical. We're from different worlds. I don't want your life. And judging by the number of telephone calls you take all day, I don't think you could move your practice here and become a part of my life." She turned away and began sponging clean the range top. "But all that is irrelevant, because even if we had grown up next door to each other, I still wouldn't want to get married."

"Well, I do. I want my child to have a name."

"He'll have one. Mine."

"I want my child, my only child, to bear my name, Laney."

"Then we'll compromise by hyphenating it or something."

"McLeod-Sargent? Sargent-McLeod? What the hell kind of a name is that to stick on a poor defenseless kid?"

"It'll have to do."

Out of sheer frustration he ran his hand through his gray hair. "You would subject our child to going through life explaining why his parents don't have the same last name, why they don't live together, why they aren't married?"

"A lot of children have parents who aren't married."

"True. But most were married at one time. Besides, just because it's almost the norm these days, that doesn't make it right."

"It wouldn't be like he had come from a broken home. He would never know anything different."

"What about dividing his time between the two of us, in two vastly different parts of the country, two different cultures? Does that sound ideal to you? That's not a decent life for a child, Laney. A child should grow up with both parents visible, a father and a mother."

"I told you you would be visible. You can see him whenever you want."

"I don't want my kid to grow up with only one parent around."

"Well, I did and I survived!"

By then both were shouting. Laney's words reverberated off the walls of the kitchen and rendered them both momentarily speechless. Their rasping breath was the only sound that remained. The air was charged with tension.

Laney was the first to look away and Deke's heart twisted with pain at the defeated slump of her shoulders. He wanted to go to her, hold her, comfort her, but he wisely kept his distance. He knew when to back off from a witness.

"Leave the rest of the dishes. I'll do them," he said quietly.

She spun around as though to argue with him, but she reeled with fatigue and he saw the argument die on her lips. Her face was wan and there were dark circles under her eyes. Deke cursed himself for driving her so hard, for forcing her to make that admission. It was a bit of history that he knew she would rather not have revealed. She nodded and left the room without speaking.

A half hour later he found her burrowed under the

covers of their bed, her knees drawn as close to her chest as possible. She was absently rubbing her stomach, where he could see the vigorous movements of the baby. He sat down beside her.

"Are you all right?"

Her look told him that his question was absurd. "Oh, yes. I'm just wonderful." She came upright, gripping the counterpane with white fingers. "A man I don't even know moved in on me and began to rearrange my house. Now he wants to rearrange my life. I won't marry you, Deke. Do you understand?"

"Laney," he said gently, and pressed her back onto the pillows. She was working herself into another lather and he was afraid she might suffer another attack of cramps. "No, I don't understand, but I won't ask you again."

Her hysterics subsided. She looked at him like a child who had just been assured that the nightmare was after all only a dream. "You won't?"

"No. Not when it causes you this much distress." His hands came out tentatively to touch her. "You're a case for the books, Laney McLeod. Another woman in your position would be framing a man into marrying her. That's what I liked about you in the first place. You're so different."

The backs of his fingers stroked her cheek. "What happened to your father?"

She wet her lips and avoided his eyes. "He died."

He could smell a lie. It was his job to be able to. And this lie Laney had just told him stank to high heaven. But for now he was going to let her get by with it. "I'm sorry I forced you to think about it. I told you once that I would never do anything to hurt you. Do you believe that?"

Her eyes returned to his. "Yes. I also believe that you'll keep pressuring me about marriage."

He smiled then, though his expression remained tender. "You're coming to know me well." Switching off the lamp, he stood.

She grasped his hand. "Where are you going?"

"To take off my clothes."

"Oh."

When he had stripped to his underwear, he joined her in the wide bed and took her in his arms. His mouth sought hers in the darkness. "Are we back to that?" he asked a few seconds later.

"Back to what?"

"Back to your shrinking and stiffening every time I hold you and kiss you. I thought we'd overcome that."

"I didn't—"

"Did you have a merry Christmas?" he asked out of context, interrupting her. His hands glided up and down her arms, over her shoulders, across her stomach.

"Your gifts were too extravagant," she chastised mildly.

She had been embarrassed by his generosity. He had bought her expensive maternity clothes, which she objected to, saying she had plenty to finish out her term. Perfume, accessories, a frothy negligee that had made her blush as she stammered a thank you, a string of pearls that even now were around her neck.

For the baby there had been a complete nursery of

furniture—baby bed, chest, rocking chair, a cradle for when he first arrived home. A huge gift-wrapped box sent all the way from F.A.O. Schwartz contained a stuffed panda bear, almost life-size, and a teddy bear that, when wound up, simulated the sounds of fetal life, including the mother's heartbeat.

"I never saw anything like this," Laney exclaimed when she unwrapped the teddy bear, impressed in spite of herself.

"They're new." Deke beamed, glad of her approval.

There was also a baseball mitt and a pair of pink ballet shoes. "For whichever," he had said, chagrined when she looked at him as though he were mad.

She had surprised herself by sneaking off a few days before to buy gifts for him. One was a sweatband to wear around his forehead when he jogged. He was a fanatic about getting in a few miles every day and had complained about sweat running in his eyes. She had also bought him a canvas sling to facilitate carrying fireplace logs. When measured against his gifts, hers looked paltry and she was almost embarrassed for him to open them. But he received them enthusiastically, kissing her soundly after opening each.

He had taken her in his arms and said, "But none is as wonderful as my other gift."

"What gift?" she asked, mesmerized by the dazzling multicolored reflection of the Christmas tree in his eyes.

"This gift." They had been sitting on the floor. He lowered her to her back on the rug in front of the hearth and laid his head against her stomach. He kissed it softly. "I think I can hear Scooter's heartbeat," he had whispered.

Now he burrowed his nose into the fragrant hollow of her neck. "I didn't ask you about the presents. I asked if you had a happy day."

She closely examined the way she had felt before their postdinner argument and decided that it had been one of the most joyous days of her life. "Yes. It was wonderful."

"Good. I wanted it to be." His lips nibbled at hers.

She was responding to his caresses now. Her body was malleable as he pulled her into a closer embrace and her arms went around his back. She sought his warmth, gravitated toward it in spite of her earlier protests. Lately her body often ignored the instructions of her mind.

When his lips blended with hers, he heard her murmur of pleasure and felt it deep in his own throat. He felt, too, the response of her mouth and the tightening of her nipples against his hard chest. His tongue beckoned to hers and they indulged in an erotic game.

He brought one of her hands from around him and pressed it against his chest. He waited, holding his breath. At first tentative, then curious and emboldened, her fingers combed through his chest hair and pressed more firmly to massage the hard muscles beneath the taut, warm skin. Every cell in his body rioted. He was about to burst into flame but knew he couldn't risk ruining everything.

Damning himself for being a masochistic fool, he eased her away. "Good night, Laney," he said hoarsely.

Her hesitation was her giveaway. He read in it the reluctance with which she turned away from him. She spoke a faint "Good night."

He adjusted himself to her, fitting her bottom into the curve made by his pelvis and thighs. He heard her soft gasp when she felt his rigid manhood against the back of her thigh, but when she didn't pull away, his arm curved around her. Under the covers, his hand slipped beneath her nightgown and smoothed over her stomach. Her hair tangled with his on the pillow. She nestled closer.

And in the darkness he smiled.

She was alone when she awoke the next morning. She sat bolt upright in the bed and for one panicked moment was afraid that he had left for good. But the closet was open and his clothes were still there, hanging next to hers. She flattened a hand over her breasts to calm her thudding heart.

Would she care that much if he were to disappear as suddenly as he had appeared?

Irritated with the answer, which flashed like a banner headline across her mind, she threw the covers back. The bedside clock indicated noon. She must have been exhausted to have slept so late.

Deke returned from jogging while she sat at the kitchen table, sipping orange juice. She had showered and was dressed in a pair of maternity jeans and a huge cable-knit sweater she had found at the army-navy store. The sleeves, much too long for her arms, were rolled back to her elbows, and the turtleneck almost swallowed her chin.

"Stand up," Deke said, grinning broadly as he came through the back door. He was dripping wet with perspiration despite the temperature outside. She was pleased to note that he was wearing the sweatband she had given him.

Puzzled, she obliged him. Taking her hands, he stretched her arms wide on either side of her body and inspected her appraisingly. "You're absolutely precious." He patted her tummy. "I love that outfit." Lifting his eyes back to hers he asked, "A kiss?"

"A shower?" she retorted, sniffing the air.

He laughed. "You've got a point." He flicked a drop of sweat from his index finger onto her cheek.

"Go!"

"All right, all right."

Laney was laughing as she put two slices of wheat bread into the toaster. She was relieved by his mood. Everything was back to normal. Last night's argument wasn't going to carry over to today.

But as the days of her vacation time dwindled and she and Deke spent more time alone together, she was held in a constant state of suspense as to when he would bring up the subject of marriage again. And he would. She knew he would.

She wouldn't marry him. That was an indisputable fact. There could be no marriage for Laney McLeod under any circumstances, especially those she found herself in.

She had no adolescent illusions about Deke's affection for her. It stemmed from the fact that she was pregnant with his baby. Nothing more. She dismissed his claims that he had pursued her long before he even knew about the baby. Perhaps he had. But that wasn't surprising either. Deke Sargent was used to winning. He wouldn't like having his trial cases dismissed on a technicality. He would have felt that her running out on him without an explanation was like that. A default. An unsatisfactory resolution. She represented a challenge to his ego. He wasn't accustomed to women sneaking away the "morning after." A man like Deke would have been compelled to go after the one woman who had.

No, he wanted her because he wanted his baby. That was the one thing lacking in Deke's life. He was professionally successful, wealthy. He had everything except someone to bear his name into the future. And Laney suspected by the hints he had dropped that he was concerned about that. He came from a large family that apparently placed importance on lineage. Deke was well into middle age. If he was going to have a family he could enjoy, he needed to get started. Laney was only the means of providing that one missing element in his well-put-together life.

He would persist in his determination that they marry. She would continue to refuse. An impasse. Then what? What would happen after the baby came? Would he—could he—take the child away from her?

She watched him as he pored over a legal brief. The heavy, cumbersome envelopes containing contracts and documents arrived with each day's mail. The firelight silvered his hair. His brows, also sprinkled with silver, were drawn with concentration. His lips were thought-fully pursed. Each unconscious gesture, each intense expression, was familiar and endearing.

Surely he wouldn't try to rob her of her child. He wouldn't execute a power play like that, would he? Then she remembered how he had bulldozed his way into her life and she knew that he would. Her blood ran cold. They would go to court and he knew all the machi-nations, all the strings to pull, all the right words to say.

He would tell the court how she had failed to notify him about his own child. He could point out her mea-ger salary. He would grant that it was sufficient to rear a baby, but to send a child to school, pay doctor bills, buy clothes, send a young person to college? It wasn't enough.

Her face must have shown her anguish, for when Deke looked up, he said her name solicitously. "Laney? Are you having those cramps again, darling?"

His voice was gentle and seemed to float across the space separating them and stroke her. His brow was wrinkled now with concern for her. He wouldn't hurt her, she insisted to herself. He had said so repeatedly. "No, I'm fine. Just thinking about going back to school next week."

Still, as the days passed in apparent harmony, she continued to worry. Then something happened that made her financial future look brighter. But it was shocking in its own right.

One afternoon, while Deke was on the telephone with one of his subordinates in New York, her line rang and she heaved herself off the couch to answer it. Deke finished his conversation first, so he was standing beside her chair when she hung up. Her eyes stared vacantly at the instrument for several seconds.

"Nothing wrong, I hope," Deke prodded.

She shook off her disturbing thoughts and absently reached to take the hand extended toward her. "No. It's nothing bad. Rather good, in fact." Then she lapsed back into her private musings.

"Laney," he said, laughing and shaking her hand as though to wake her up. "Am I going to have to pry it out of you?"

"Oh, sorry. That was a Realtor in Tulsa. I had put my mother's house on the market when I left. I told the realtor I was in no hurry to sell. All the furniture is still there. She called to say she had showed it to a couple several times and they're ready to sign a contract."

"That is good news."

She tried to smile but didn't succeed. "Yes."

"Come here." He drew her down onto the sofa. "What's bothering you?"

She looked away, annoyed with herself. "It's silly. I wanted the house to sell, of course, but . . ."

"Is your mother dead, Laney?"

"Yes," she said, whipping her head around and staring at him in confusion. "You knew that, didn't you?"

"I assumed it when you told me you had no family. But you've never spoken of her."

"I haven't?" she asked in a thready voice. "How strange."

He pondered that a moment as he studied her. "When did she die?"

"Almost two years ago."

"How?"

She pushed her hair back with a shaking hand. "We thought she had an ulcer. It turned out to be . . . something worse." Her hand fluttered around her throat. "She died only a few weeks after she went into the hospital."

He squeezed her hands. "You don't have to sell the house if you'd rather not. Why don't you let me call the Realtor and tell her to put it on ice for a while until you feel better about it?"

Her initial impulse was to say yes to his suggestion. But common sense interfered. If Deke should try to gain legal custody of her child, she would need the money the sale of the house would bring. "No, no," she said. "I'll never live there again. It's best to sell it. The Realtor wants me there on Saturday."

"I'll drive you."

"I'll drive myself."

"I'll drive you."

"The shrubbery needs pruning," Laney remarked as they pulled into the driveway of the home she and her mother had shared as far back as she could remember. It was in an older section of the city. There were cracks in the sidewalks and the pavement was pockmarked.

Her nerves were frayed to the breaking point, and seeing the house had almost made them snap. Deke had been resolute about driving her to Tulsa. She wished she had come alone. If she became emotional, she didn't want him to be a witness to it.

"I heard the Realtor say the buyers had already hired someone to restore the yard," Deke said, looking through the windshield at the house.

"Yes. They're eager to move in."

"You can't blame them for that. They paid cash."

Laney was still dazed by the events that had taken place in the realtor's office only an hour before. The retired couple had met her there, cash in hand. The papers had already been drawn up and were ready to sign. Deke had studied them with the thoroughness of an attorney and nodded his approval. But when he saw the shattered look on Laney's face, he took her aside and whispered, "Sign them only if you want to, darling. It's not too late to back out."

"No. I'll sign them."

The buyers wanted to buy the appliances and any pieces of furniture Laney wanted to leave in the house. He had been career Army and they had moved all over the world, accumulating very little furniture themselves.

"The sale includes everything in the house," Laney said. "But I'd like to walk through it to make sure no personal items were left behind. Then I'll return the key."

Now she wished she hadn't insisted on even that condition. She dreaded going into the house, though she wasn't sure why. Her feet were leaden as Deke escorted her to the front door and unlocked it.

The interior was shadowed, gloomy and silent in the way of vacated houses with all the drapes drawn. The atmosphere was funereal and dank and oppressive.

WORDS OF SILK   125

Laney had remembered the rooms as being larger than they actually were. She walked from one to another, glancing around, touching nothing.

Her bedroom was empty save for the furniture. Everything she had wanted, she had taken with her when she left. Her mother's bedroom had been cleared as well. Laney had done that a few weeks after her death. All of her mother's clothes and belongings had been donated to a charity.

After the dismal tour she stood once again in the entrance hall, looking forlorn and disoriented. "There's nothing here you want, Laney?" Deke asked, breaking the silence for the first time since they'd entered the house.

He was amazed. There had been no exclamations of delight over an object that brought back a fond memory, no poignant tears. He and his brothers and sisters had raided the attic on a recent visit to his parents' house. It had been an afternoon of reflection and hilarity as discarded treasures were rediscovered. Laney, however, seemed a stranger to this house.

"No," she said. "Nothing."

It occurred to Deke then that the house was more than empty. It was hollow. It was like a movie set. Everything was properly arranged, but it was two-dimensional. It had no depth, no personality, no nucleus, nothing to hold it together. "What about all the personal things, memorabilia, family photographs, things like that?"

"There were no photographs. Mother didn't own a camera."

"There are no pictures of you as you were growing up?" His incredulity couldn't be masked.

She looked at him with a flare of defiance. "We didn't go in for sentiment."

What kind of mother didn't collect hoards of pictures of her child? "Maybe your grandparents . . ." he ventured.

"I didn't have any. No one. Only mother." Restlessly she began to prowl the living room. He stalked her.

"When did your father die?"

"I was little. I don't remember."

"Your mother supported the two of you alone. That couldn't have been easy. What kind of work did she do?"

Her insides were coiling tighter and tighter. She didn't want to answer any of his questions, yet he tracked her footsteps doggedly. "She worked in the credit union of a big company."

"What was she like?"

"Like?"

"Yes, what kind of person was she?"

She rounded on him. "Why are you asking me all these questions?"

"I want to know. What was your mother like?"

"About my size. Brown hair, blue—"

"I don't mean physically, I mean her personality."

"Personality?" Why was he following her around the room this way, peppering her with questions?

"Was she a happy-go-lucky sort? Melancholy, stern, frivolous, intellectual? What was she like?"

"She was my mother!" she shouted at him. "That's all, just a mother."

"And you loved her."

"Yes!"

"And she loved you."

She froze, her hands tightly gripping the back of a wing chair with a seat cushion that sagged with age. "Yes," she managed. "Of course she loved me. I was her little girl."

He saw the white knuckles, the tense lines of her face. He was pushing and he knew it, but it had to be done or Laney would forever be held by some kind of tragedy to the prevailing sadness in this house. "What happened to your father?"

"I told you he died."

"Of what? When?"

"I don't remember!"

"Surely your mother mentioned him from time to time, told you stories about him. She didn't remarry. She must have loved your father very much to hold fast to his memory all those years."

She licked her lips with a virtually dry tongue. "She . . . she didn't talk about him much."

"Do you think that's natural? Why do you think she didn't talk about him much?"

Agitated, she shoved away from the chair and flew to the window, gripping the drapes with lifeless hands. "How should I know?"

"You know, Laney. Tell me why your mother didn't talk about your father."

"That was a long time ago. What does it matter?"

"It matters. Tell me."

She spun around and her eyes were glassy with emotion. "She didn't talk about him because she hated him. She got pregnant and he married her out of duty. But as soon as I got here, he left. Vanished. He deserted us. She never saw him again. I never knew him. Now, there, are you satisfied, Counselor?"

Her hair was a wild tangle around her head and her breasts were laboring with each breath. Her arms were held rigidly at her sides and both fists were clenched.

"I'm sorry, Laney. That must have been terrible for both you and your mother."

"Go to hell," she said tightly, giving him her back and flinging open the drapes. It was getting dark outside and that only added to the morbid feel of the house. "You found out what you wanted to know. Now leave me alone."

He couldn't. He had gone this far. They had made progress, but they weren't at the source of her anxiety yet. He hated himself for being so thorough, but he had to be. "So your mother, since she didn't have anyone else, poured out all her affection on you. She lavished you with love."

"Yes."

"You were the apple of her eye."

"Yes," she said more loudly.

"She told you frequently how much she loved you."

"Yes," she screamed.

"She demonstrated what a wonderful thing it was to love and be loved, is that right? She fondled you and hugged you and kissed you every day."

"Yes, yes, yes." She spun around to face him once again.

"You're lying, Laney."

She sucked in her breath. "No. No, I'm not."

"I think your mother was embittered by what your father did to her. I think that instead of showering you with love she held you responsible for all her hardships." He advanced toward her, keeping his voice level. "I think she blamed you for coming along and ruining a budding relationship with her young man."

"Stop it," Laney cried, and clasped her hands over her ears.

He came closer, matching his steps to his words, like hammer blows on a nailhead. "I think you loved her because she was your mommy. You wanted her to love you back but she never did. Or if she did, she guarded against telling you. I think you wanted to throw your arms around her and hug her every day, but you knew she wouldn't like that. You learned that hugging and holding are invasions, violations of one's private space."

"Stop!" She was pounding her fists against her thighs. Tears were rolling down her cheeks. "She took good care of me."

"Physically, yes, she provided for you. But there's more to parenting than that. You wanted her to touch you, didn't you, Laney, to cuddle you against her breasts, to caress you?"

"Yes," she sobbed. "I mean *no*. You're confusing me."

He shook his head. Tears were in his own eyes. "No, my darling, you're getting unconfused."

She thrust out her hand, palm toward him. "Stop. Don't come any closer to me."

"I'm going to hold you, Laney, for all the times your mother didn't."

"No! I don't want you to."

"Yes you do. Don't you?"

"No, no." She groaned and pitched forward, sobbing uncontrollably.

He was there to catch her. His arms encircled her and tightly held her to him. "Yes you do," he murmured into her hair. "Yes you do."

Mechanically her hands clutched at his clothing. She wadded handfuls of his shirt between her fingers. He loved it. The tears she was crying now weren't tears of agony but healthy, cleansing tears. Cupping the back of her head, he pressed her face into his neck and rested his chin on the top of her head. "You poor baby," he intoned. "So lovable and so unloved. God. You precious girl."

She sank into the strength of his body. "Deke?"

"Yes, love?"

"Deke?" She couldn't quite believe that he was really there, holding her. Loving her.

He placed a finger beneath her chin and tilted her face up. She made a whimpering, desperate sound before clasping his hair between her fingers and dragging his face down to hers. Her lips yearned upward toward his. "Love me, love me."

He hissed a blasphemous curse that stressed his surprise and joy. He lowered her to the floor. The carpet smelled of age and dust, but they didn't notice. Laney reached for him with every straining part of her body. Mindful of her condition, he lowered himself beside her carefully but no less fervently.

He pulled her to him and cemented their mouths together while their hands battled to gain the most ground. His hands scaled her back and slid below her waist to cup her hips and press her into his hard passion. She adjusted herself to him willingly and their sighs of ecstasy echoed across the still room.

Her hands fumbled with his heavy overcoat and he shrugged it away impatiently. Fingers usually dextrous stumbled over each button of his shirt as she worked them free of the holes. Then her palms glided over his bared chest and stomach and the springy hairs tickled and thrilled her.

He pulled her coat away. As his mouth feasted on hers his tongue plunging deeply, he opened the buttons of her dress and found her breasts.

"Oh, yes," she moaned, and arched higher to him.

Clumsily he struggled with the clasp of her bra until it came undone and freed her breasts for his mouth. Then, with gentle hands and fevered lips and finessing tongue, he caressed her and brought her nipples to peaks. She made small crying noises as they frantically adjusted their clothing. Their movements were frenzied, their breathing labored. Then the rasp of his zipper was the only sound as they were held in a suspended silence laden with anticipation.

Slowly he lowered himself over her. "What if I hurt you?"

"Please, Deke." She slid her hands into his open shirt. Bravely she touched his flat brown nipples. Deke gritted his teeth.

Her dress and slip were bunched around her waist.

He felt for her tenderly. The nest of dark golden hair was lush and silky and he let his fingers nestle in its promise until she moaned with gratification and growing need. He palmed the soft mound and his fingers searched downward. When he found her melted warmth, he positioned himself between her thighs.

He introduced himself into that sweet heat with infinite care. He barely breached the threshold, but it was enough of his fullness to reduce her breathing to shallow gasps. His movements were slow and precise. Deftly he stroked only what he knew needed to be stroked to bring her to completion. His own need was to bury himself as deeply and as snugly inside her as he could. He fiercely ignored that desire and concentrated only on bringing joy to one who had had so little of it.

"Oh, God, it feels so good," she whispered on ragged breaths.

He smiled down on her rapturous face and dipped his head. "I'm glad. To me too." His tongue found her nipples taut and flushed and it laved them thoroughly while the velvet tip of his stiff manhood worked its slow, delicious magic.

Laney knew she was slipping into that sublime oblivion that he had guided her to before. She didn't want to go alone and she had enough presence of mind left to know the sacrifice Deke was making for her. Forgetting any remnant of shyness, she slid her hand between their bodies where they were joined.

His heart nearly burst. Her name was a groaning sigh on his lips as her fingers encircled what he wouldn't impose on her. Her hand made it almost as good for him as being inside her, and when he saw her face suffuse with light and her body began to quicken around him, he let go of that grueling discipline. He tensed and shuddered and let his love pour into her.

Long moments later she opened her eyes to meet his liquid-green stare. "What happened to me?" she asked throatily.

He lifted a tousled blond strand from her cheek and rubbed the silky hair across his lips. "I loved you. And you loved me back. And it was wonderful."

CHAPTER | 7

I t's beginning to snow. We'd better go." They were lying facing each other, her cheek against his chest. Legs were entwined and arms were wrapped around each other. Deke hated to break that closeness, but the roads would become hazardous if they didn't try to beat the storm back to Sunnyvale.

"All right." Laney disengaged herself from his embrace.

The next few minutes were awkward as they re-arranged their clothing. They were like two who had survived a tragedy and didn't want to be held responsible for the way they had behaved during the crisis. They couldn't quite meet each other's eyes.

Laney was mortified that once again she had begged him to make love to her. Deke was afraid that he had ruined their tenuous relationship by once again taking advantage of her emotionally unstable condition.

Laney locked the door behind them and they stumbled through a fierce wind and icy pellets of sleet and snow to reach his car. "Oh, the key," she said.

"We'll mail it back." Deke hustled her into the car. They drove in silence while he negotiated the treacherously icy streets. After having driven east for half an hour they edged ahead of the storm and the highway was dry. He could turn more of his attention to Laney, who was sitting silently, staring out the window.

"Laney?"

"Yes?"

"What are you thinking?"

Sighing deeply, she looked at him. "All my life I blamed my father for deserting us. I grew up thinking he must have been a terrible person. But now I don't know. He was probably just extremely unhappy. Maybe my mother didn't love him and he knew that. Maybe he just felt trapped and had to get out or go mad."

"Sweetheart." He reached for her hand, brought it to his mouth and kissed it.

"I think I've done him a disservice. Some of the blame has to belong to him, of course, but I never once analyzed his side."

"You can see the situation now from an adult's perspective."

"But why couldn't I see the whole picture before? Why didn't I realize what Mother was doing to herself? She was always so bitter. She never let herself be happy."

"Nor you."

"Nor me," she admitted. "Why didn't I see that and rebel?"

"Because children instinctively love their parents. Even abused children defend the parents who abuse them."

"She didn't abuse me."

"There are all kinds of abuse, Laney. You suffered the psychological kind. The marks your mother left on you are invisible."

"But you saw them," she said quietly.

"And we'll work on healing them. By example you learned to guard against displays of affection. I intend to teach you otherwise."

She rubbed her stomach. "I'll tell him every day how much he is loved. Hold and fondle him." Pensively she returned her gaze to the virtually deserted highway. Only occasionally did another pair of headlights slice through the darkness. "I don't think Mother knew she was doing anything wrong. You called me a sad lady once. She is the truly tragic figure in this piece."

Deke was less forgiving. "Laney, do you blame me for making you see her for what she was?"

Her eyes were glistening as she looked across the interior of the car and said, "No, Deke. I thank you."

The car left the highway so quickly that at first Laney thought they had blown a tire. Deke switched on the emergency blinker and slid across the plush upholstery to take her in his arms.

"I didn't want to put you through that ordeal, but I had to break down the barrier I knew was there." His hands held her face and his thumbs alternately drifted over her lips. "Consider it a kind of shock therapy."

She lowered her eyes. "And the other? Was that therapy too?"

He waited to answer until she raised her eyes once again to his. "No. That was because I wanted very much to love you, and have since I came to the schoolyard that day. For twenty-seven years you've been deprived of loving. I wanted to give it to you in its most splendored form. It was a distinct privilege to be able to give you what you needed most."

He kissed her then. His tongue entered her mouth only far enough to touch the tip of hers. Laney felt the caress throughout her body because it reminded her of his lovemaking. She knew from that moment that she would always miss him when he wasn't there. Her groan as she dragged her mouth from his wasn't generated by passion but by a feeling of hopelessness. "Deke, you're making me need you and I don't want to. I'm afraid to."

"That's a fear instilled by your mother. You know that now, Laney."

"Yes, but knowing its source doesn't make the fear go away."

He hugged her hard. "We'll hug and kiss that fear away. Get used to needing me. I intend to make myself indispensable to you. And to Scooter." He bent his head and planted a sound kiss on her stomach.

For the first time that day she laughed. "Is that what you're going to call the baby once it arrives?"

He raised his head and winked. "Only if it's a girl." He delighted in the rich sound of her laughter, but he wasn't fooled. He saw the violet bruises of fatigue ringing her eyes. "You're tired, aren't you?"

"Exhausted."

He returned to his side of the car and drew her across the seat. "We've got a long drive. Stretch your legs out. Would you rather lie down in the backseat?"

Her eyes wandered over his face. "No. I'd rather stay by you."

He made a gruff sound in his throat as he brought his mouth down to hers. This time the desire that hadn't yet been quenched was unleashed. He kissed her hotly and deeply, his passion tempered only by his knowledge that she was tired. He regretfully raised his head and touched her dewy lips with his fingertip. "Go to sleep."

She nestled against him, laying her head on his shoulder. When his hand came around her and rested on her stomach, she covered it with her own.

That night heralded a significant change in their relationship. Laney began to trust him in bits and pieces. They didn't speak of it, but her increased trust hovered on the horizon like a glimmer of hope. Each day they drew closer to the beacon.

She went back to teaching school the first week of January. Deke stayed busy at home. He was working on a particularly involved case and was carefully preparing his defense. Via telephone he was constantly in touch with his client and with his assistants, who were doing massive amounts of research. Nightly he pored over the briefs, making hasty notations in the margins with a furiously scrawling pen. No detail escaped him;

yet, every time Laney inquired, he was vague about the date set for the trial.

She realized how frustrating it must be for him to work in unfamiliar surroundings. "You should be in New York, shouldn't you?"

"I should be here with you," he said, lifting his attention from a stack of papers he was studying.

"You know what I mean. I'm sure these conferences with your client would be much more beneficial in person than over the telephone. You need reference books that aren't here, so you have to wait until the next day and have someone else—"

"I know all the problems, Laney. I save the most explicit cussing for when you're at school." His attempt at humor failed.

She felt fat. She was tired of her legs cramping and her back hurting. She was tired of being bludgeoned day and night from the inside. The sight of maternity clothes made her sick to her stomach. She resented the svelte models in fashion magazines.

Everything irritated her. The picture frame on the opposite wall was hanging crookedly and she was too apathetic to get up and straighten it. One of her pupils had broken her fingernail that day by dropping a box of crayons on it. She hated her waddling gait. And she was probably destroying a brilliant lawyer's career.

More than she wanted to admit, she was worried about what would happen after the baby was born. Deke would leave her. He would be tired of the game by then. And when he was gone, she would miss him.

She almost wanted to hurry his departure so she wouldn't have to dread it anymore.

"Go back to New York, Deke, where you belong," she said crossly. "I can't have you sacrificing your work to stay here with me. I'll call as soon as I feel labor pains. You can be here within hours. If you want to be. Frankly I think any man who wants to escort a blimp around is crazy."

He got out of his chair and squatted down beside her where she lay on the couch. He took her hand and pressed it between his. "Who would go to childbirth classes with you?"

"You weren't here the first six months. The instructor acted as my partner."

"And that battle-ax never let me forget it either," he said smiling, remembering the first night he had gone with Laney and the severe dressing down he'd received for his prior negligence. "Dr. Taylor has appointed me deputy in charge of making sure you don't get too tired."

"That's another thing," she said testily, snatching back her hand. She knew she was whining, she knew she was acting bitchy, but she couldn't stop it. Let him haul around the load she carried for just a few hours and see what kind of mood he'd be in. "I'd appreciate it if the next time we go for a checkup the two of you wouldn't talk as though I weren't there. I may be bloated and pregnant, but I still have my mental faculties."

He only laughed and drew her close. "You're in a great mood tonight. Why don't you go take a hot bath before bedtime?"

"All hippopotamuses enjoy soaking, don't they?"

His lips showed amusement, but he knew better than to laugh. "Go on. You'll sleep better."

She grumbled and groaned, but she heaved herself off the couch and went into the bathroom. She was drying off when Deke opened the door. He knocked once but then pushed his way in, afraid for her safety because she had been in there so long. He had a fear of her slipping in the tub.

Steam swirled around them as they stared at each other in mutual surprise.

"You're very beautiful, Laney," he said thickly. Even swollen with his baby, her body attracted him more than any other woman's.

It would have been senseless to reach for a towel to cover herself. So she stood there and let his gaze travel over her nakedness. She didn't believe them, but she latched on to his words. They were what she needed to hear. "You still think I'm beautiful?"

"Very. Did you think I didn't?"

"You haven't . . ." Unable to finish her sentence, she looked away.

"Made love to you?"

She shuddered. "You don't have to explain."

"I didn't want you to think I expected it just because of what happened in Tulsa."

"I'm embarrassed by what happened."

He came to her then and placed his hands gently on her shoulders, willing his eyes to remain on her face and not take in the delights of her feminine form. "You responded to me as the passionate, generous, sensuous woman you are. For the second time. You've nothing to be ashamed of or to apologize for."

She swallowed hard and her voice was small when she said, "I thought my aggression might have revolted you."

He laughed then, a hearty, low, rumbling laugh that vibrated in her ear as he pressed her cheek against his chest. "Hardly, my love. Hardly," he whispered earnestly. He held her for a moment, then set her away from him. "Are you finished in here?"

She was slightly breathless from their embrace. There was something naughtily exciting about being naked while he was fully clothed. The contact of her skin with the varying textures of his clothes had ignited tiny sparks of desire all along her body.

"I, uh, rub this lotion on my stomach every night," she said, wishing her heart would slow down. "It's supposed to help prevent stretch marks."

"Go lie down on the bed. I'll do that for you tonight."

He joined her on the soft linens a few minutes later, wearing only his underwear and carrying the bottle of lotion. She hadn't seen the need to put on a nightgown, since he would have to grapple with it to smooth on the lotion. Only the soft amber glow of the bedside lamp clothed her. She wondered at her lack of modesty, but not enough to want it back. Somehow such bashfulness seemed silly now.

"Have I ever told you that I like your hair?" she asked as he poured a generous portion of lotion into his palm and then began to rub it into the tightly stretched, itchy skin of her abdomen.

"Gray hair? You have a penchant for old men?"

"You're not old! When did it start turning gray?"

"When I was about twenty-five. My father's was the same way. His hair was completely white by the time he was fifty." His hands were talented in the art of massage. They applied just the right amount of pressure, and Laney felt her fatigue and querulousness disappearing beneath their soothing touch. Her eyelids became heavy and she was almost asleep when he said, "All done."

"You didn't do my breasts." Her eyes popped open when she realized what she had sleepily mumbled. Deke was looking at her curiously. "Never mind," she said quickly. "I can skip a night."

He caught her hands as she tried to pull the covers over her. "You rub this lotion on your breasts?"

She wet her lips with her tongue, having no idea of the sharp stab of agony her unconscious action brought to Deke's loins. "Breasts can get stretch marks too."

"We can't let that happen," he said with a trace of lechery. He poured another dollop of lotion into his hands and rubbed them together sensuously. He laid them on her breasts simultaneously and Laney closed her eyes and held her breath as supremely blissful feelings flowed over her at his touch.

His hands were warm and slick with the lotion as they kneaded her. Her breasts filled his hands. They were lifted and pressed and lightly squeezed with slippery motions as the lotion lubricated her skin. His strong, lean fingers made shallow indentations in the creamy flesh.

"I wish you had assigned me this job weeks ago," he said huskily. The dusky tips of her breasts had responded to the flirtation of his fingertips. Forgetting his original purpose, he plucked at them gently until they hardened between his lightly pinching fingers. When she made a gurgling sound that might have been his name, he sought the tender buds with eager lips.

When his mouth surrounded her, Laney arched off the bed and imbedded all ten fingers in his thick hair. He entrapped one nipple with a gentle sticking motion and rolled his tongue over it until she was writhing beneath him. Her arms went around him and her hands refamiliarized themselves with the corded muscles of his back, the supple groove of his spine, the indentation of his waist and the taut leanness of his buttocks.

"Oh, God, Laney, I want you again," he whispered against her breast, rubbing it with his lips. "Do you remember what it's like, darling? Do you remember how it feels when I'm inside you?"

"Yes, yes," she breathed. She remembered all too well and her body did too. It was longing for him to fill her again.

His hand smoothed down her side, along her thigh. It curved around the top of her leg, which was still slender despite her pregnancy, and trailed up the silky inner side. He outlined the fleecy delta and touched her with infinite intimacy. "I kissed you here. Do you remember? And here."

She sighed. "God, yes. I remember." She rolled toward him slightly, thrusting her hips against the solid ridge of his masculinity.

With a desperation that bordered on savagery, he lifted himself to kiss her mouth. It was a reckless, hot, voracious kiss, and they drew on each other as though they were starved. Laney could almost fed his blood boiling in his veins.

Then suddenly he rolled away from her onto his back. His teeth were clenched and he cursed as he peeled off his underwear and hurled it away. His chest rose and fell like a bellows. Every muscle in his body was bunched with the control he exercised.

When his breathing was somewhat restored, he turned to face her. His expression was tender as he outlined her lips with the tip of his index finger and erased the worried frown he saw there. "We can't, Laney." She stared at him in hurt speechlessness. "You know how much I want to." Still she didn't speak.

Taking her hand, he drew it to his sex, which was still hard and surging with life. He pressed her hand to it. "I want you. But the next time we make love I want it to be perfect. I don't want to have to hold back, worrying that I might hurt you or harm the baby. I want more than just an orgasm for both of us. I want intercourse of the body and of the spirit. I want that same feeling of oneness that we had that night in New York. Strangers until then, but so familiar with each other that it was like coming home." He touched her cheek. "Do you understand?"

She did. Her eyes were shining with tears as she nodded her head. "Yes, I do."

Taking her hand away, he kissed it first, then her mouth. He pulled the covers over both of them. Long after he had turned out the light and Laney had felt the soft rhythm of his breath against her shoulder, her body continued to feel full and expanded. It had nothing to do with pregnancy. It wasn't a physical sensation, but rather one of the soul. Something akin to joy, to love, was bubbling inside her like a smoldering volcano about to erupt. She savored the feeling. It frightened her, for it made her vulnerable. But it was too delicious to wish away.

"Things are progressing a little faster than I had predicted," Dr. Taylor told them the next afternoon. Deke had picked her up from school—he was driving her to and from the schoolyard these days because he didn't want her driving alone—and they had gone straight to the doctor's office for her appointment. "I think you may deliver early."

Deke squeezed her hand and she smiled at him timorously. "There's nothing wrong, is there?" she asked the doctor.

"No, no," he answered broadly. "You haven't gained a lot of excess weight; yet, it's a very large fetus."

"Laney isn't in danger, is she?" Deke asked, spearing the doctor with eyes that had made trial witnesses shiver with dread.

"No, but I want her to be extremely careful from now on. Rest with your feet up as much as possible after you come home from school. Don't get over-tired." He looked at Deke and cleared his throat. "You probably should abstain from, uh . . . you understand."

Both Deke and Laney blushed, remembering what had happened the night before.

"Of course," Deke said with the solemnity of a penitent boy in Sunday school.

"I'll see you next week," the doctor said, dismissing them.

If he had thought that his caution would make life easier for Laney, he was wrong. His warnings made life unbearable. Deke hovered over her like a mother hen. He would hardly let her brush her own teeth. He drove her to distraction about being careful at school and even took to parking across the street during her recess periods so he could watch her while she was outside. He ignored her petitions for him to stop.

After three days of this she left her students in the charge of one of the other teachers, who was highly amused, and marched across the street to confront him. Yanking open the car door, she said, "Deke you're being ridiculous. Everyone thinks you're insane, including me."

"Why did you lift that kid onto the seesaw, Laney?"

She stamped her foot in exasperation. "Aren't you listening to what I'm saying?"

"Is that coat heavy enough? I don't want you catching a cold."

"All right, you asked for it."

"Where are you going?" he demanded, opening the door after she had slammed it shut and mutinously started back toward the building.

"I'm going to call the police."

"And tell them what? That your husband is concerned about your well-being, even if you're not?"

"I'm going to tell them that there is a pervert in a trench coat lurking around the elementary schoolyard. I may add that he has a funny Yankee accent. That'll get them here fast, believe me."

He had returned home from jogging just minutes before her recess period. He had unthinkingly thrown on his trench coat as he raced from the house. Now he looked down at his naked legs sticking out of a four-hundred-dollar coat and stifled a laugh. "A flasher? You're going to tell them that I'm a flasher?" He began to unbelt his coat, and when the belt was free, he caught the sides in his hands and threw them wide.

Laney gasped in shock and then relief. He had on a pair of running shorts and a T-shirt beneath.

Deke bellowed with laughter. "Scared you, didn't I? Come here, you." He wrapped the coat around both of them as he drew her against him. "The only person I'm going to expose myself to is you," he growled in her ear. "As soon as I get a chance."

She breathed in the scent of his citrusy cologne and healthy perspiration. "I still think you're a fool."

"You're right. Where you and Scooter are concerned, I behave like a man with no sense whatsoever. That's a peril of fatherhood, I'm afraid. You'll just have to put up with me."

He put up with her and for that he should have been canonized. After the incident with the trench coat he did refrain from going to the school, but he still dogged her every move, which irritated her to no end. She didn't feel well. Her movements reminded her of a walrus, as did her shape. And Dr. Taylor repeated his warnings and instructions until she wanted to scream at him.

Deke bore the brunt of her bad humor. He bore it with admirable forbearance. The only thing that raised his temper was her constant nagging that he shouldn't be in Arkansas when he had a major trial coming up in New York.

"I don't need you to remind me of my responsibilities, Ms. McLeod," he said acerbically when she broached the subject one evening after a particularly arduous day. It was late February and the weather was cold and rainy. She had been forced to stay indoors with twenty-six hyperactive students all day.

"I was practicing law before you got to high school," he added, and returned to his notes.

But Laney was spoiling for a fight and wouldn't let it drop. "You're cheating your client. I don't want that on my conscience."

Deke slammed a book down on the coffee table and came to his feet. The flames in the grate were reflected in his eyes. "I've never cheated a client in my career. I give each one the best defense I can."

"You've postponed the trial date three times!" she shouted. "I've heard you on the phone. What is your excuse?"

"A completely valid one. That my wife is having a baby and I can't get away at the moment."

"I am *not* your *wife*."

"I'm glad you brought that up," he said. He rounded

the coffee table and came within inches of her. "I don't want my baby born a bastard, Laney."

She recoiled at the ugly word. "D-don't call him that."

"That worries you, does it? Well, you'd better worry about it, because that's what the rest of the world will dub him. Is that what you want for your child?"

"No! Of course not."

"Then marry me."

"I can't." Her hands were wringing each other.

"Why? Because your mother was pregnant when she got married and your father bolted?" He took a step closer and his voice became persuasive rather than abrasive, silk rather than burlap, "That was them, Laney. They have nothing to do with us."

"I told you from the beginning I'd never marry you. Why don't you just accept it?"

"I don't want to." His temper flared again and he couldn't contain it. "What makes the thought of marriage to me so hideous? Night after night we lie together naked in each other's arms. We tease each other with caresses until we're practically frothing at the mouth, until we want to make love so bad we're nearly senseless. Yet, we don't stop the foreplay because it feels so damn good."

"Don't talk to me like that!"

"Why? Because talking about it keeps it from being a shameful secret? Makes you face up to what's what? Rids you of those blinders that are as much a part of you as your thumbprint?" He took a deep breath, but it did little to calm him. "The times we've been together have been pure magic. I can't wait for the next time, and by God, if you'll admit it, you can't either. We're compatible. We rarely argue over anything except this subject. I'm financially solvent. We both want what's best for our child, which is a family environment with two parents. So what's your problem, Ms. McLeod? Huh?"

His arrogance infuriated her. "What's yours? You've spent forty-two years as a bachelor. Why do you insist on marrying me all of a sudden? Are you afraid you won't find anyone else? Or am I just a convenient baby machine who's going to provide you with the one plaything you don't already have?"

"That's not true and you know it." His jaw clamped tightly and he pushed the words through a fence of teeth. "You're afraid to chance loving anybody. You're a coward."

"I'm—"

Suddenly she went very still. Then she extended her hand to him as she bent double. "It's my water."

Deke called on every deity in heaven as he led her to the nearest chair and dropped to his knees beside her. "Is this it? Should I call Dr. Taylor?"

She nodded just as a pain knifed through her vitals. Deke saw her face go white, felt her breath stop. He gripped her hand until the contraction subsided. Oddly her concern was for him. He looked ready to collapse. She touched his cheek. "Call the doctor," she said softly. "Then we can go to the hospital."

She never remembered the next half hour clearly. Deke was shouting into the telephone, cursing answer-

ing services in general and making rude suggestions as
to what the operators could do with their switchboards.
In a flurry Deke got her bag, which had been packed
for weeks, and they put on their coats, found the keys
to one of the cars—both sets of keys had disappeared—and painstakingly made their way to the car.

Deke drove like a madman. "It's too early, isn't it?
How early? Laney, are you in pain? How early?"

"Three and a half weeks."

"Three and a half weeks! Almost a month!"

"Deke, would you please stop shouting. I may have
gone into labor, but I have not gone deaf."

"Oh, God, three and a half weeks," he groaned as
though she hadn't spoken. "That damned quack. I never
thought he knew what he was talking about. I know you
think I'm just saying that now, Laney. But I never took
his word on anything. I'm gonna kill him."

Laney started laughing and he whipped his head
around, fixing her with wild eyes. "Actually I'm
pleased," she said. "At least now you can't back out of
claiming it's yours."

"Very funny, Laney. Very— Oh, God, another pain?
Hold on, darling."

Through a mist of pain she saw the lights of the hospital looming in the windshield, and never was there a
more welcome sight. Deke had gotten her there without
smashing them into any obstacles. She was put in a
labor room while he took care of having her checked
in. When he joined her he flew into a rage and summoned the head nurse.

"What kind of room is this?" he demanded. "It's

small and dark. Laney is claustrophobic and this room looks like a cell on Devil's Island."

"I'm sure your . . . uh . . . Ms. McLeod will be fine, Mr. Sargent." He could have slapped her then for the knowing tone in her voice. "This is the only labor room available, and—"

"You're not listening," he ground out. "I want her out of here. I'll go through every damn room in this hospital until *I* find her one that's bright and cheerful. Got it?"

The nurse got it, with stern-lipped disapproval and mutterings about obscene rudeness, but she got it. Laney was moved into a room with wide windows and rows of fluorescent lights. Deke stormed at the nurses; threatened Dr. Taylor with malpractice for his inaccuracy and tardiness when he sauntered in a half hour behind them; and paced. But to Laney he was solicitous and loving.

Her labor progressed through the night and he was beside her the whole time, holding her hand, spooning ice chips through her parched lips, talking to her softly, going through the exercises they had learned at their childbirth classes.

It wasn't quite dawn when Dr. Taylor told them it was only a matter of minutes and went to scrub. Deke moved to her side and took both her hands. "I called you a coward. God, I'm sorry, Laney. You've been so damn brave."

"It hasn't been bad. You've been here."

His eyes were strangely glossy as he leaned over her. "Laney, marry me before the baby is born. I summoned a minister out of bed. He's been outside the room for hours, waiting for me to get up my nerve to ask you again. Please, if you have any feelings for me at all, let me give my child my name."

Amidst the pain and the medicinal smells and the twisting agony of her insides, she began to laugh. "Deke, how like you." Then a pain gripped her and they counted through it together while a nurse announced that it was time to go to delivery.

Laney looked up and said weakly, "You'd better get your preacher in here fast."

Seeing the look on his face was worth the pain she was suffering. A blinding light as brilliant as any of her pains seared her brain, and with it came the realization that she loved him. It almost didn't matter that he would soon leave her. For right now he was with her and she would seize this moment and treasure it.

Deke rushed to the door and brusquely summoned the minister.

"This is highly irregular," the nurse said nervously as the man was pushed inside the room. "If Nurse Perkins finds out—"

"Just keep your mouth shut and she'll be none the wiser," Deke snapped. "Think what an interesting tale it'll make. Well, hurry up, Reverend, she's about to deliver."

The poor man fumbled and stuttered through the ceremony. They had to pause once while Laney suffered a gripping contraction. When the minister called for the ring, Deke slipped a huge diamond on her finger.

"Where did you get that?"

"Tiffany's."

"In New York?"

"I brought it with me. Are we done?" he asked the minister.

"I now pronounce you man and wife."

"Good." Deke kissed her hard.

"She really shouldn't wear that ring into the delivery room," the nurse said, pushing the gurney toward the door.

"Here, keep this until we come out," Deke said, thrusting the ring at the befuddled minister. "I can trust you not to steal it, can't I?" Deke winked at him as the door swung shut behind them.

"Well, I was thinking I would have to come get you," Dr. Taylor said from behind his mask as she was wheeled into the delivery room.

Laney couldn't quite register it all, but she knew Deke was there with her, encouraging her, shouting his delight when the doctor held up a squirming, squalling baby boy. "He's a perfect specimen," the doctor reported.

Laney let her body sink gratefully onto the table while everyone went about the routine tasks of an event that is nonetheless miraculous. She was marvelously content, tears of joy silvering her lower lashes, when Deke was allowed to lift her son so she could see him better.

"He's beautiful," she sighed.

"Beautiful?" Deke roared. "He's . . . he's . . . *beautiful!*"

A nurse took the infant to footprint and weigh him. Deke clasped Laney's hand and was lovingly staring down into her face when he saw her eyes go wide and her teeth bite down on her lower lip.

"Darling?" he said with mounting panic. "What is it?"

"Ohhh," she wailed in agony. Her head lolled against the table.

"Dr. Taylor," Deke shouted. "Something's wrong!"

CHAPTER | 8

Kevin Todd Sargent slept in the hospital nursery bassinet, knees drawn up under his tummy, fanny in the air, head turned to the left, oblivious to everything, including the adoration being heaped on him . . . and his sister. Amanda Lea Sargent's lips pursed and she made a sucking motion with a perfect rosebud of a mouth. Her father squeezed her mother's shoulder and laughed softly.

"You scared the hell out of me just before she was born." He pressed Laney close to him and shivered when he recalled those terrifying seconds when he had seen her face contort with pain. Dr. Taylor had still been attending her between the high stirrups over which her legs were draped.

"Nothing's wrong, Mr. Sargent, unless you have an aversion to twins."

Mandy Sargent had been a surprise to everyone. Because of the crowding of her brother, who was five ounces heavier and an inch longer, her heartbeat hadn't been heard. Mandy had made her entrance into a totally unsuspecting world.

"I apologize," Laney said with the kind of serenity granted exclusively to new mothers.

Deke Sargent pressed his lips to his wife's temple and said, "Apology accepted." He kissed her. "Ready to go back?"

"No. I love looking at them."

"But you need all the rest you can get while you're here in the hospital. That's twelve pounds of baby you were carrying around, my love."

She groaned and massaged her flatter, though still spongy, stomach. "Don't remind me. I'm so glad they're where they are now rather than where they were."

Deke laughed out loud, to the annoyance of the head nurse, who still regarded him as a troublemaker. "So am I." Gently he steered Laney back toward her room, the largest maternity suite the hospital offered. He made a comical picture as he teetered, trying to match her baby steps with his long legs.

Entering the room, Laney spied a modest bouquet of carnations. They were flanked by the elaborate arrangements Deke had provided. "Did you thank Mr. Harper for the flowers when you called him?"

"Yes." He eased her down on the bed and helped her lift her legs, folding the covers over them with great care. "He said for you not to worry. They've already found a substitute to finish the rest of the year."

"But, Deke, I want to go back. I can teach the last six weeks at least."

He was already shaking his head. "For Godsakes,

don't be such a martyr. You've just given birth to twins. One baby would be hard enough to take care of properly while you were teaching. Two babies would be impossible. You couldn't help it that you had to take off sooner than you planned because the babies were early. Now, that's all I want to hear about it. Do you want some more custard?"

She made a face. "No, but a cheeseburger and fries sounds delicious."

He leaned over, grinning conspiratorially. "Tomorrow for lunch I'll sneak in the greasiest cheeseburger basket money can buy."

"And risk getting all four—my God, *four*—of us thrown out of here? Nurse Perkins nearly had a billy fit when she caught us drinking champagne."

"How else is one to celebrate the birth of twins? That broad has no soul." Sitting on the edge of her bed, he took her hands. "Have I told you thank you?"

"About a thousand times."

He wasn't the least abashed. "I'll say it every day of my life. They're wonderful, Laney."

"I know." She let her head rest heavily on the pillow in well-earned but pleasant weariness. "For more than half my life I thought I couldn't have a child." She looked at him then and her eyes were filled with unshed tears. "Can you imagine how happy I was when I learned I was pregnant? Dismayed, yes, and worried about what it would mean to my job, but elated that I was to be given a child after all. And now, two!" She laughed in spite of her weeping eyes. "I thank you, too, Deke."

"You're so sweet." He leaned over her and touched her lips with his. It was a brief kiss, tender and dear.

When he drew away she said, "I can pity Mother now. My father should have been there with her when I was born, as you've been with me."

Deke laid a hand along her cheek. "I've been thinking about that." He paused, not wanting to upset her. "As you know, I have access to records and files, by fair means or foul. I could start tomorrow trying to locate your father if you want me to. I can't promise that we'd ever find him. He may be dead. But I'd give it a hell of a try."

Her eyes drifted to the large window that overlooked the front lawn of the hospital. A setting sun gilded the winter landscape. "It occurred to me when Mother died that I had no living relative that I knew of. It's a panicky feeling, that you're a solitary person in a world built around families. I suddenly wanted to find my father or learn what had happened to him.

"But I decided then, and I still feel, that if he had wanted me in the first place, he would have stayed at least long enough to develop some kind of kinship with me. He may be someone I'm better off not knowing. And if Mother was responsible for his leaving, if he was just a miserably unhappy man, he probably has another life now, another family. I would only be an unwelcome intrusion to remind him of an unhappy time in his life. I wouldn't want to be that."

She brought her eyes from the window to the much brighter glow in Deke's eyes. "Thank you for offering, Deke, but no. I think it's best to start with Todd and Mandy as my family."

"And me?"

She looked down at the diamond on her left hand. "You forced me into marriage, you know. I thought shotgun weddings were for the poor bride's benefit."

"So did I. But in this case the bride has a warped view of a lot of things."

Laney still couldn't classify how she felt about being Mrs. Deke Sargent. She had sworn never to be Mrs. anybody. She had sworn never to love. But she did. And she was terrified because she did.

Her emotions were too fragile now to bear examination, so she changed the subject by holding her ring hand at arm's length and studying the glittering facets of the marquise solitaire. "It really is an outrageous ring."

"It's downright vulgar. I was trying to impress you."

"Sweep me off my feet?"

"Something like that."

"Like hell. Sweeping is too subtle. Exploding, imploding, steamrolling, is more your style."

"I'm a mover and a shaker?"

"Definitely."

He grinned. "I'm a man who gets quick results, though, don't I?" She smiled back and he thought she'd never looked more beautiful. "Are you too uncomfortable to be kissed?"

"You kissed me a few minutes ago."

"No, not like that. I mean a *real* kiss. One like this."

He aligned his lips with hers. Though the kiss conveyed all the tenderness he felt, it was potent, his tongue dipping repeatedly into her mouth. His arms went around her and lifted her up to cradle her against his chest. She slipped her arms over his shoulders and held him fast, surrendering her mouth to the mastery of his.

"Excuse me," the frosty voice said from the door. They pulled apart and saw Nurse Perkins looking at them with the distaste she would have bestowed on a spilled bedpan. "We're bringing the babies in now. If you're staying, Mr. Sargent, you'll have to put on your gown and mask."

With a broad smile designed strictly to irritate her, he said, "I'm staying."

The house would have made Bedlam look serene.

It was crowded. Deke had purchased one more of everything, disregarding the fact that not all the furniture would fit into the second bedroom. One of the chests had to be placed in the hallway. A second teddy bear with the recorded fetal sounds had promptly been ordered from New York. *And what did they need with two panda bears?*

"Yeah, but Todd gets the baseball glove and Mandy gets the ballet shoes."

Thank the Lord for small favors.

Laney had talked him into giving away the flowers to other hospital patients so they wouldn't have to cart them home. He had obliged, then filled their bedroom with a veritable tropical garden. Upon her arrival home, among the flowers, the stacks of disposable diapers, dispensers of cotton balls and wet wipes, hampers of receiving blankets, cans of baby powder, jars of Vaseline, tubes of diaper rash ointment, bottles of antiseptic solutions and boxes of still-wrapped gifts, she could barely locate the bed.

Their third day home proved to be her undoing. Mrs. Thomas had rearranged the bedroom a dozen times, trying to maximize the space. The nursery was hopeless. One had to wedge oneself between the furniture to get to the babies.

Throughout the day there had been a parade of visitors, mostly the teachers from Laney's school. She got the distinct impression that they had come to ogle Deke rather than to see the twins. They simpered and postured and gushed and made naughty insinuations pertaining to his virility. Laney wanted to vault out of bed, slap them and instruct them to keep their hands off her husband; then she wanted to knock Deke on the head for smiling like a Cheshire cat even as they drooled. Though covetous glances were directed toward her ring, no one paid any attention to *her*.

She hated herself for succumbing to self-pity and crying harder than the babies, but that was what she was doing when Deke came into the bedroom after having waved their last visitor off.

"Laney!" He was alarmed and rushed to the bed. "What's the matter?"

"Everything," she blubbered. "Everything. I have a pounding headache, but everyone's too busy to bring me an aspirin and I don't have the energy to get up and get it myself. You're either on the telephone or courting those scavengers of the divorce courts. Mrs. Thomas has hidden everything I own. I can't find my hand lotion. And I'm still fat," she wailed on a dying note and buried her face in the pillow.

Deke went to the bedroom door and shouted down the hallway, "Mrs. Thomas, take care of Todd and Mandy for an hour. I don't want to take any calls. This bedroom door is to remain closed under all circumstances except fire or flood." He slammed the door and came back to the bed.

"Go away," Laney mumbled as his knee made a deep crater in the mattress. Then: "What are you doing?"

He scooped her off the bed and carried her to one of the rocking chairs, which had been moved into their room. "My sister warned me about postnatal depression."

"You told your family about me? About us?" She let him settle her in his lap as he sat down in the rocker.

"Didn't you think I'd share that kind of news with my family? They're thrilled and can't wait to meet you and the babies. Now relax. Still got a headache?"

"A little one."

"Here?" He slowly moved his fingers over her temple.

"Uh-huh."

"Cold?"

She yawned and snuggled closer. Her hand rested over his heart. She loved the steady feel of its beating against her palm, loved the chest hairs that peeked out of the V of his collar to tickle her nose. "No. I'm warm now," she said drowsily. "I don't think I've ever been rocked in a rocking chair before. I like it."

"So does Mandy. She told me so last night."

Laney smiled.

When she woke up, she was lying in bed. At first she thought she was seeing things. The room had undergone a transformation. The flowers, save for one yellow rosebud on the bedside table, had been removed. All the baby paraphernalia had been collected into a large plastic laundry basket. Everything could be easily seen and reached but was no longer scattered about. Her cosmetics had been neatly arranged on her dresser top, as they had been before she left for the hospital.

Deke stuck his head through the door. "Awake?"

"Yes. How long have I been asleep?"

"A mere hour." He held out her robe. "Why don't you shower before dinner?"

"That would feel good. What are the babies doing?"

"Sleeping. You've got plenty of time to eat before their dinnertime."

At the door to the bathroom she turned. "Deke, how did you know . . ." She waved vaguely toward the room.

"My sister, God bless her. I called and begged for advice. She said she remembers all that clutter and the confusion of coming home from the hospital with a new baby. Said her world seemed to have been invaded. Her suggestion was that I restore things as close to normal as possible."

"She's going to think I'm a fool and a heartless mother."

He laughed. "Oh, no. You were the heroine to be pitied for having an unfeeling, insensitive clod like me around. Need any help in the bathroom?"

She pulled the edges of her robe together and shook her head. "No, thank you." She was more self-conscious of her body now than before. It was no longer swollen with pregnancy, but she thought her stomach looked like bread dough, and her breasts seemed to sag to her knees.

He wanted to tell her otherwise, that he thought she was beautiful. But he only smiled and said, "When you're done, I'll serve you dinner."

He did, but not in the manner she expected. When she came out of the bathroom, having showered, shampooed and dressed in a modest but gorgeous silk dressing gown Deke had bought for her, she wordlessly stared at his handiwork.

He had set up a small table in the bedroom. On it was a linen tablecloth, a small cluster of flowers, two lighted tapers and two place settings already filled with the food Mrs. Thomas had prepared. Soft music was playing on the portable stereo.

"Deke!" Laney's heart expanded with pleasure. Overcome, her eyes filled with tears. "This is lovely."

He hugged her tight. "You deserve it after five days of hospital food and then the riot this household has been in."

He seated her with the gracious flair of a maître d'. "Milk!" she exclaimed, laughing. In her wineglass was milk rather than the deep ruby burgundy that shimmered in Deke's.

"For the babies." His hair shone silver in the candlelight and his straight white teeth gleamed behind his smile. Under his appreciative gaze she felt feminine and attractive for the first time in weeks. He raised his wineglass. "To my beautiful bride of one week. To the mother of my son and daughter."

Shyly she responded to the toast with her milk and they sipped at their glasses while staring at each other over the rims.

"I have a present for you."

"After a candlelight dinner, there's more?"

It was late. The small table had been removed hours before. Mrs. Thomas had left for the evening. Laney sat propped on pillows in her bed. She was replete with good food. Getting up and walking through the house with Deke after their meal had helped relieve the tight soreness between her thighs. Her son sucked noisily at her breast. His sister was curled against her other side.

Deke set the large gift-wrapped box on her thighs. "Can you open it with one hand, or would you like me to open it for you?"

"You open it." Todd tended to have a temper tantrum if a meal was late or interrupted.

Deke, with melodramatic suspense and a poor imitation of a drum roll, opened the box and took out a thirty-five-millimeter camera complete with flash device and extra lenses. He presented it to his wife on outstretched hands.

Laney stared at the camera for long silent moments.

Then she reached out and touched the camera, lifting her eyes to Deke's. She didn't have to say anything. He had known what significance the gift would hold for her. His own eyes grew misty as she brushed her fingers across his lips. "Thank you."

"Our kids are gonna be so photographed that they'll have perpetual purple and yellow spots dancing in front of their eyes," he said, and she laughed. "Every day of their lives will be chronicled if you want it to be. In years to come they'll know how much we loved them from the very beginning." Before she could start crying again, he extracted the booklet of operating instructions. "But first I have to learn to work the thing."

She appreciated his lighthearted mood. All day she had either been weeping or on the verge of tears. Her emotions were running high. This security, this sense of belonging, of needing and being needed, was something she had never expected to have in her life. She was like someone who had grown up in the desert and had been suddenly transported into a rain forest. These new emotions were too foreign to assimilate.

Up until a few months ago, she had been totally alone. Now she was surrounded by three people whom she loved. Would they love her back? That was the gamble, wasn't it?

Her babies would. As Deke had said, children instinctively love their parents, especially their mothers. Deke? She watched him as he pored over the instruction booklet and studied the dials on the camera. He was so very beautiful. Kind. Generous. Good-natured. But did he love her? He never spoke of love.

They had consciously avoided the subject of the future. Heretofore every reference to it had been "When the baby is born," "Until the baby . . ." But now what? They couldn't go on living in this tiny house, which had been crowded with two. Deke couldn't continue practicing law via telephone and the postal service. Something would have to happen. Whatever that something was, Laney dreaded it.

But tonight she didn't want to think about it. Tonight she wanted to bask in this tiny slice of light. Up until now her life had been bleak.

Todd was done. But as she tried to move him away, he thumped her breast with a tiny fist and began sucking again. Laney laughed with maternal delight. The white light on the camera flashed and she looked up to see a jubilantly grinning Deke. He appeared quite pleased with himself.

"That's *numero uno*." He focused again.

"You shouldn't be taking pictures of me like this." She worriedly glanced down at her bare breast.

"Why not? You look beautiful."

She had wound her hair into a topknot after her shower. It had softened and loosened by now. Wispy strands had escaped to frame her cheeks and lie on her neck. Her skin was rosy and glowing in the subdued light. The silk robe was a perfect foil for her softness. Deke had chosen the color because it had reminded him of the blue-gray sea color of her eyes.

He snapped several pictures in rapid succession as she cupped Todd's head and lifted him away from her breast. He screwed up his face in momentary discontent, then burped and settled against her arm like a sated despot.

His parents laughed indulgently. "Give the little pig to me." Deke set the camera aside. "Todd, don't you know you've got to save some milk for Sis?" he addressed the sleeping infant.

Laney raised her daughter to her other breast. Deke was temporarily dazed by her graceful movements as she plumped her breast in her hand and guided the roseate nipple toward Mandy's waiting mouth. He felt like a deviate at a peep show and cursed the thickening behind the fly of his jeans.

"I'm relieved to hear you calling him by name," Laney remarked. "I was afraid he'd go through life as Scooter." When he didn't say anything for a long time, she lifted her head and caught him staring at her. His eyes were fixed on Mandy's angelic face pressed against her breast.

"That night in the elevator, before the blackout, did you notice me?"

His question surprised her and she wasn't sure how to answer. She hadn't been in the habit of man-watching. She had always felt there was no point in initiating something that wouldn't go anywhere. Unlike most modern women, who weren't afraid to express a frank interest in an attractive male, Laney had rarely let herself even look.

"I didn't pay much attention to men in general. You know why." She wet her lips. "But yes, I noticed your hair. And your clothes."

"My clothes?" He laughed shortly. "That's interesting. I was mentally stripping yours off." She blinked rapidly in disbelief. He leaned forward and whispered, "Couldn't you tell?" She shook her head. "We've never talked about that night, Laney."

"I'm not sure we should."

He was certain they should. "Remember when I took your jacket off?"

"Yes. Was that necessary?"

His brow wrinkled. "In retrospect, maybe not. *Then* it seemed necessary, or maybe I was just trying to come up with an excuse to touch you." His voice slipped down a note. "I unbuttoned your blouse."

"I remember." Her throat almost closed around the words.

"The heel of my hand accidentally rubbed against your breast. I barely touched you. It lasted no longer than a heartbeat. But I heard your breath catch in a little gasp. That was the sexiest sound I'd ever heard in my life. That was when I first began to want you."

She stared at him, her eyes wide. "I never knew that. I swear that when you carried me into your apartment, I was barely cognizant. I had no idea—"

"Laney," he said, touching her cheek, "you don't have to defend yourself. I was the seducer, not you. I knew you weren't fully aware of what was happening. But it was happening all the same." He removed the pins that held her hair. It spilled over his fingers like beams of light "When you took your clothes off, I almost had a heart attack."

She turned her face into his palm, embarrassed. "Why did I do that?"

"I think your subconscious was pleading with you to make yourself available to love. You never had before. You wanted someone to look at you and discover that you were desirable. And you were, you were." His voice was but a husky murmur against her cheek. "I thank God you chose me for your initiation. I wanted so badly to touch you, to hold your body against mine. You tasted so good. All of you. You don't still blame me for that night, do you? Do you remember that I offered to stop?"

"Yes." Her confession was a soft moan as his lips flirted with the corner of her mouth.

"But I don't honestly know if I could have stopped, Laney. Once our bodies were that close, once I had sampled your mouth, your breasts, caressed you, I don't think I could have stopped for any reason. I simply had to have you."

"I wanted you to make love to me."

"Ah, Laney." He pressed his forehead against hers. He squeezed his eyes tightly shut. His breath misted her face. "I'm so damn glad to hear you finally say that."

They both realized what it had meant for her to make that confession. She had wanted and needed him then. She had reached out for him. It was possible that she would want and need him again, now and in the future. To Laney it was a giant leap toward trusting. To Deke it was a small step toward gaining her confidence. They were now going in the same direction and not pulling against each other.

Deke didn't gloat over his victory, but kissed her with infinite care. This wasn't a moment for passion. It was promised, but it would have to wait. Before pulling away, he pecked a series of light, rapid kisses on her face to relieve the emotions that had welled up inside them. "If it weren't for that ten-minute blackout in New York City, the world would be without Todd and Mandy. Think what a shame that would be."

"Yes, just think." Laney appreciated his unspoken understanding. He knew she wasn't in any state, physical or mental, for romance. She lifted Mandy from her breast and blotted the milk-sticky lips. "That should hold them for a few hours anyway."

"Here." Deke leaned down to take his daughter in his free arm.

Laney kissed the top of each baby's head. "Can you handle both of them?"

He frowned down at her as he straightened, bearing both his children in the crooks of his elbows. "Just watch me and see. You stay put. I'll tuck them in."

She watched him walk away, her heart thrumming with love for all of them. "Deke?" she asked hastily.

"Yes?" He turned around to face her.

"Are you coming right back?"

He took a long time in answering, letting her know by the radiance of his eyes how glad that simple question made him. "I'm coming right back" was his soft response.

CHAPTER 9

The telephone rang as Deke unlocked the front door. They had been on their first outing with the twins. It had amounted to no more than a drive through town, but Laney felt like a convict released from prison after years of incarceration.

With Todd clutched in his arms, Deke ran to answer his business line. "Hello." He hugged the receiver between his chin and ear. "Yeah, we've been out. What's up?"

Laney laid Mandy in the portable crib they had placed in the living room. She kicked free of her blankets almost faster than her mother could unwrap her. As Deke continued to fire pertinent questions into the telephone, Laney retrieved Todd from his father's arms and laid him down beside his sister. No sooner was he free of his outdoor trappings than he set up a howl for his lunch. Mandy, content up to that point, heard her brother's distress, decided she must be suffering, too, and started wailing.

"I'm sorry," Laney mouthed as she rushed toward the kitchen to warm two bottles. Deke waved off her apology and covered his other ear with his hand. She rushed back to carry first Todd, then Mandy, into the bedroom. She changed them while the bottles were warming.

Deke was just hanging up the phone when she came through the living room again, carrying the two bottles toward the bedroom. He looked grim. "Something wrong?"

He forced a smile. "Business as usual. We'd better get them fed."

He got to Todd first and placed the plastic nipple in his mouth. Laney took Mandy and together they migrated toward the living room, each taking a corner of the sofa. The twins were several weeks old and the household had more or less settled down to a routine. Mrs. Thomas was taking a day off.

"They're getting so big." Laney lovingly examined Mandy's dimpled hand. "Next week they go in for their first-month checkup. I can't believe it's been that long."

"We might have to cancel that appointment, Laney."

The low, level tone of his voice sent a cold shaft of foreboding through her. She raised her head to look at him. "Why?"

"We'll be in New York by then." He rushed on before she could say anything. "That was my senior assistant on the telephone. I had asked for one more postponement for the trial, but the judge denied it. We go to trial Monday."

"The day after tomorrow?"

"Yes. I guess we'd better call Mrs. Thomas and see if she can come in this afternoon to help us pack. I'll make our airplane reservations, call the landlady, see about—"

"Objection, Counselor." Mandy flinched at the emphasis in her usually lulling voice. "I'm not going to New York tomorrow."

Deke seemed to count to ten slowly as he wiped away the dribbles on Todd's chin. "I'm sorry it has to be with so little notice. I didn't want it to be, but that's the way it is and there's nothing I can do about it. We'll pack only what's essential to move the twins. The rest we can get at home."

"*This* is home."

He ignored her interruption and continued. "When this trial is over, we'll come back and see to the house and furniture. The trial shouldn't take more than a few weeks. By that time we will have picked out a house. I think you'll like Connecticut. I've had realtors scouting out possibilities."

"I see you've got the details all worked out," she said tightly.

"I wish I could give you more time, Laney."

Mandy had finished the bottle. Laney placed the infant on her shoulder and patted her back until she burped.

"Time has nothing to do with it, Deke. I'm not going. Nor are my babies." She left the couch and exited the room, going into the twins' room to lay Mandy gently in her baby bed. She curled into a ball and fell fast asleep.

Deke laid Todd down, and after he found his fist to gnaw on, he, too, fell asleep. Deke caught up with Laney in the hallway. "You're my wife. They are my children. We're a family. Where the father goes, the family goes."

She halted her striding journey into their bedroom to spin around and confront him. "Where have you been, Deke? Under a rock? That might have been true a hundred years ago or even fifty years ago, but it doesn't hold true in today's society." She continued on to the bedroom, took off her cardigan and hung it in the closet.

"You surely don't expect me to give up my practice in New York," he shouted.

She whirled on him. "No. But you obviously expect me to give up *my* job. I happen to like this house very much. I don't want to leave it and move to an unfamiliar part of the country that I don't anticipate liking."

He cursed and peeled off his sweater, something which Laney wished he hadn't done. It left his chest bare down to the faded, frayed fly of his jeans. They rode an inch below his hair-whorled navel and made his masculinity all too evident. She turned her back.

"Look at me, Laney." Defiantly she faced him again, but kept her eyes at some point above his head. "This has nothing to do with jobs or houses and we both know it. It has to do with your fear of commitment. You're still afraid to trust me, aren't you?"

"Don't analyze me. Ever since you pushed your way into this house the first time, you've been analyzing me like a bug under a bell jar." Because he was so close to the heart of the matter, she began to pace. She unbuttoned the first few buttons of her blouse to relieve the constriction around her throat. "I was coerced into marrying you."

"No one was holding a gun to your head."

"I didn't want to marry you because I knew something like this would happen. I knew I would become a possession, like a piece of furniture you could move or rearrange or put into storage as the mood struck you. Well, I'm not, Deke Sargent. I was doing fine on my own before you came along."

His fists thumped his thighs as if he would love to smash something. "What about the babies?"

"I can't believe you'd even consider moving them now. They're much too young."

"I concede that it won't be easy, but babies fly in airplanes and ride in cars all the time. We'll hire Mrs. Thomas to travel with us and send her back on the next return flight if it will make you feel better about flying with them."

"It's not just the traveling. It's . . . they're too young."

"You're not breast-feeding them anymore, Laney."

She glared at him then. "Is that why you encouraged me to wean them early and put them on formula? So I would be ready at the drop of a hat to move to New York?"

He taught her a whole new dictionary of expletives as he stamped around the room, raking his hair with his fingers. "Do you actually think I'd do that? Do you think I'd risk the well-being of my children on a selfish whim? God!"

He slammed his fist into his other palm. "I wouldn't have cared if they suckled you from here to New York City in sight of everybody. I thought that was beautiful. The reason I wanted you to agree to Dr. Taylor's suggestion to put them on formula was because I could see how breast-feeding was depleting you. It was costing your body plenty to feed them. Todd is a glutton and neither of them was getting enough milk. It was better for everyone."

She knew he was right, but she didn't want to acknowledge it. "They need to be here with their own pediatrician."

"We can take your medical records with us. There are thousands of qualified doctors in New York."

"We're back to that again." She paused for emphasis. "I don't want to live in New York City."

"I told you I'm looking for a place in Connecticut. It's lovely and not so different from here. My family lives there."

"But for a while we'd have to live in your apartment. I don't want my children exposed to the streets of Manhattan."

"They're babies!" he laughed incredulously. "They're not going to be out on 'the streets.' Besides, New York's not nearly as dangerous as people make it out to be. Those reports of bad things happening to innocent people are exaggerated."

Her eyes lifted to his and they were as cold as the North Sea and just as turbulent. "Oh? Look what happened to me."

His face changed by degrees. The cockiness faded as

her words gradually seeped into his brain. Never had Laney seen such a furious visage. Her spine prickled with fear and she took a step backward.

It did no good. He advanced on her, taking three long strides. His hand went to the back of her head, wound her hair around his fist and hauled her against him. He finished unbuttoning her blouse, yanked it from her body and flung it to the floor. Now they were hip to hip, belly to belly, breast to breast and breathing like marathon runners.

"Apparently you don't remember that night correctly at all," he drawled. "At least not the way I remember it. The way I remember it, you weren't a victim, Laney, but an all-too-willing participant. You begged me for it."

With each word his head had descended until with the last one he crushed her mouth with his. His tongue pushed through her lips to plunder rapaciously. His hand tightened its grip on her hair, forcing her head back for his conquest. His other arm closed around her to hold her while his hips ground into hers, punishing.

But as quickly as the violence erupted, it was tempered. He made a strangled noise in his throat and his mouth gentled. Instead of plundering, his tongue now persuaded. His hand let go of her hair to rub her shoulders, to slide to the clasp of her brassiere and unfasten it. He massaged the silken skin of her back and flexed his fingers around her now slender waist. Then he wedged his hand into the waistband of her jeans, past the elastic band of her bikini panties, and, caressing the smooth flesh of her derriere, pulled her tighter against his hard passion. The soft jeans did nothing to defuse its power.

Taking his lips from her mouth, he kissed an ardent path to her ear. His breath was rasping and hot. "Laney, why do you make me say things like that?" He drew his hand from her jeans, but kept his rampant manhood nestled in the V of her thighs. "You make me angry because you refuse to see reason." His hands squeezed her waist lightly, then coasted up her rib cage to caress her breasts. "I love you, Laney." He nuzzled his face in the curve of her neck as his thumbs found her nipples. "I love you."

"You always know the right words to say, don't you, Counselor?"

He stiffened. Pushing away from her abruptly, he looked into her face, and what he saw he hated.

"You think you're very clever, don't you?" she asked. She picked up her blouse and pulled it on with quick jerking motions. "You think you've got me all figured out. Tell her you love her and she'll fall into your hands like a ripe peach. Is that what you think?"

He remained stonily silent.

"Ever since I met you in that elevator, you've run roughshod over me, first by taking advantage of my hysteria."

"Oh, hell," he hissed. "Are you going to fall back on that? Haven't you absolved yourself yet? It was one night of indiscretion out of your whole life, Laney. Join the rest of us sinners! You don't have to use hysteria and being tipsy as excuses for doing what you damn well wanted to do. If we had met under different circumstances, the result would have been the same. I would have wanted to take you to bed, and I think you would have gone. Now, dammit, don't blame me again for comforting you when you needed it or hold me responsible for things getting out of hand," he roared.

Wetting her lips, she strove for composure. "Granted, your first motivation might have been kindness. And I accept responsibility for what happened after I went into your apartment." With a lift of her chin she said brazenly, "I don't regret having had sex with you. I got Mandy and Todd from that. But you ramrodded your way into my house, my life. You browbeat me into marrying you so our children would be legitimate. Now you think you can woo me into doing your bidding with soft words and silken phrases."

"Are you finished?"

"Not yet." She drew in a shuddering breath. "You're right about one thing: When I was young, I would have given anything on earth to hear my mother say she loved me. But even if she had, the words would have been empty, just as yours are. I was no more than a fixture in her life, and I think that's the way you see me too. You want to put me into one of those neat little compartments of your life and leave me there until you're ready to take me out and play with me."

"That's not true, Laney."

"Then why haven't you given me one single choice in this whole affair? There is more to loving than having sex every night and saying pretty words. It's giving a person freedom, making her feel worthy, letting her choose to love back."

"All right," he said, slicing the air with his hands. "That all sounds very nice, but it's bull and you know it. I'm not going to argue theory with you, or psychology. I'm sick and tired of it, if you want to know the truth. And I'm just a little bit sick of having to handle you with kid gloves."

"Then don't handle me at all."

He released a sigh and raised his hands in defeat, letting them slap his thighs as he lowered them. He stared at a spot on the floor for a long time, gathering his thoughts. When at last he raised his head, his face was openly imploring.

"I haven't known your kind of heartache, Laney, because for as long as I can remember I was surrounded by a loving family who gave me confidence. However, I can sympathize. I know you're scared."

"I admit it. I'm scared."

"Why? Why hold steadfast to that fear when you've come so far? You took tremendous strides when you left that mausoleum of a house and began a new life after your mother died. The way you feel about your father now shows that you've accepted that part of your life, but you're not going to let it defeat you. You've come to trust me a little." He reached out his hand. "Come with me, Laney. Take that final step. Let's commit ourselves to each other."

She stood on the rim of a chasm. She didn't want to go back where she had come from. Deke stood on the other side, holding out the promise of happiness and love. But between them seethed all her fears. Crossing that churning gulf was too chancy a risk to take. She might fall, get sucked under. She wanted him, but she wanted him where they were now, where it was safe, where there were no demands or commitments.

"I'm not the one leaving," she cried in self-defense. "You're deserting me just like my father did my mother."

"I have no choice. You know that."

"That's probably what he said to her."

Deke's outstretched hand fell to his side and dangled there lifelessly. Did she think no more of him than that? Hadn't he gone about as far as a man could go to make her happy? If she still refused to accept that happiness, what more could he do?

"You want a choice?" he asked in a voice as deflated as his spirit. "I'm giving you one. I have to return to New York tomorrow. When this trial is over, I'm coming back. I'm packing up Mandy and Todd and taking them home with me. Since you don't believe that I love you, you can *choose* at that time whether to go with us or not. But my children are going with me."

The house was dismally empty without him. Even with the clutter and noise of two healthy infants and the bustling activity of Mrs. Thomas, Laney walked through the house like a visitor to a museum, detached, looking but not touching. It reminded her of the house in Tulsa.

Deke telephoned several times a day to check on the twins. More often than not he spoke to Mrs. Thomas. When he and Laney did converse, they were coolly polite. She inquired about the trial and he asked for details on the babies' progress. They discussed nothing personal.

After she got a "Go ahead, but in moderation" from Dr. Taylor, she began to exercise like a fiend, doing sit-ups until she was afraid she would rupture something. The day she could zip into her tightest pair of jeans, she clapped her hands and whooped so loudly that both twins were startled out of a morning nap.

The weather turned warmer, and when Laney thought it was safe, she and Mrs. Thomas drove the twins to the school to let her former class view them. To the curious questions about Deke, she simply responded that he had returned to New York for an important trial.

She tried to busy herself around the house, but actually there was little to do. When she suggested to Deke that she really didn't need Mrs. Thomas every day, he cut her off peremptorily and indisputably stated that the housekeeper stayed. He had already expressed his concern over Laney staying in the house alone at night, so she dropped the subject of Mrs. Thomas out of fear that he would hire a live-in.

She filled her days with caring for the twins, but basically she was idle and lonely. Mr. Harper called to ask her about the next fall semester. She hedged, telling him that she didn't know if she was going to teach or not.

"Can I tell you later? In August, maybe?"

"That's a problem. We like all our contracts in order by the middle of June. You'll have to let me know by then."

So now she had one more thing to think about during the long hours of the night. They were the worst to endure. She lay in the bed she had shared with Deke and missed having him there beside her. She missed him so much, she ached. It was an ache that ate into her marrow.

If anyone had told her she could be that lonely with twins to take care of, she wouldn't have believed them. She had expected her children to fill her life to overflowing. But they didn't fill the void that Deke had left behind. Each day she found herself growing a little more apathetic about her life. That shocked her—panicked her, in fact. Had that happened to her mother? Had she not loved Laney because no one had been there to love her?

Perspiring, Laney sat up in bed with a startling insight. It made sense. When one wasn't loved, one didn't have much love to give. Was she then not being fair to her own children? Would she unknowingly deprive them as her mother had deprived her?

She was in the kitchen the next morning when the telephone rang. It had been a sleepless, miserable night, and she had been relieved to finally see the sun come up. Mrs. Thomas had arrived and was gathering laundry. The twins had been fed and bathed and were sleeping.

She stared at the telephone for a moment before answering it. Her heart began to pound. "Hello."

"Good morning."

The words fell on her ears like golden drops of honey, pure and warm and sweet and sensual. She remembered the first time he had said those words to her, the first morning she had awakened in his bed. He had been a stranger to her then, but no longer. Now he was her soul.

"Good morning."

Without preamble he said, "I think the case will go to the jury Thursday afternoon. In any event we should have our acquittal by Friday." She smiled at his characteristic overabundance of confidence and hugged the telephone receiver tight. "I'm going to say this only once Laney. I'm coming down there this weekend. I want you to have everything packed." He hesitated and then said forcefully, "I'm moving you and the twins to New York."

"Like hell you are," she said into the telephone before gaily dropping it back into its cradle. She jumped up with a broad smile on her face. "Mrs. Thomas," she shouted. "Help me pack!"

The housekeeper huffed into the kitchen. "Did you say pack?" Her face was wreathed in smiles. "Then he's coming to get you?"

"No. I'm running to him. Don't answer that!" she exclaimed as the telephone began to ring again. "Don't answer it for the rest of the day. Come on, we've got a lot to do."

While Mrs. Thomas attacked the drawers that held the twins' clothes, Laney made airline reservations. In an hour and a half, miraculously, they were ready to leave. Mrs. Thomas recruited her husband to drive them to Tulsa in Laney's station wagon. They would keep it parked at their house until further notified. Deke had relinquished the rented Cadillac when he returned to New York.

At the departure gate, after their bags had been checked, Mrs. Thomas broke down in sobs, realizing for the first time that "my babies," as she put it, were leaving. Laney knew that she was included in the term of endearment.

"You won't forget to call Deke, will you?" Laney was afraid that her plan might backfire and she would be left standing alone in LaGuardia Airport with two infants.

"No. As soon as I see you take off, I'll call him on that WATS line number," she blubbered. "Flight 345 arriving in New York at five ten."

"Yes, and be sure to leave a message if he's in court. Thank you, Mrs. Thomas. For everything."

She hugged the tearful woman, promising to see her soon when they returned to settle the house and furnishings. Then, with a flight steward carrying Todd, she rushed aboard the aircraft before she could change her mind.

The twins were angel-kissed that afternoon. At least they behaved perfectly on the entire flight. Laney fed Todd because he was the more rambunctious eater, while a delighted flight attendant fed Mandy her bottle. Both slept after that.

Laney almost wished they would be contrary. Then she wouldn't have time to weigh her decision, to think about the enormity of what she was doing, to worry over Deke's response to it.

Suppose he didn't meet them?

Of course he would. He wouldn't want his children to be stranded at the airport, even if he felt like choking their mother. After all, she had hung up on him and hadn't answered again, although the phone had rung a good hour after she had abruptly ended their call.

But what would he be feeling?

At the sound of his voice that morning, Laney had realized what a colossal fool she had been. She wanted him, she needed him and she loved him. She had been stubbornly clinging to a fear that belonged in her past, before Deke. Her mother had been bitter, angry and disappointed with the world; she had not had the ability either to give or take love. Laney had realized that she would become like that, too, if she didn't take a chance on giving her love away.

No one was going to come to her door passing out happiness. Nor was it enough to merely find it. One had to take that last step, to reach for it. That involved risks, but it was either a matter of taking the risks or forever living with a gnawing emptiness inside.

She had been selfish too. Even if Deke didn't love her, he loved his children and would make a happy home for them. In good conscience she couldn't deny them that. Nor did she want to deny herself.

If only he meant . . .

"Fasten your seat belt please, Mrs. Sargent. We're on our final approach."

Nervously Laney latched the safety belt and checked the twins. How did she look? Were her clothes wrinkled? Did she need lipstick?

Her stomach was in her throat and it had nothing to do with the landing. Would he notice that she had lost those last five pounds? What if he was angry? What if he had been called out of court? What if she had made him lose his case?

It was too late to back down now. The airplane taxied to the gate and the door was opened. Women with young children were allowed to disembark first.

Todd announced his arrival in the Big Apple with a gusty bellow that his sister soon echoed. "Oh, Lord," Laney said as she hoisted one of the diaper bags over her shoulder and carried her son into the jetway. An attendant followed with Mandy.

Over the throng Laney saw Deke's gray hair first. His eyes were trained on the door through which they had to pass, and he spotted them immediately. Besides, Todd's bawling was hard to miss.

Deke began elbowing people aside as he waded through the crowd clustered in the waiting area. He looked distinguished and austere in his dark three-piece suit. She could read nothing in his expression. Just as he reached them, his face split into a huge grin.

"Wait, Deke!" Her stern tone halted him and wiped the smile off his fade. She had to know. It took more courage than she knew was in her, but this was the moment of truth and she had to ask this question now or forever wonder. "Did you mean it when you said you loved me?"

Their offspring screamed in indignation because they were in unfamiliar and uncomfortable surroundings. They were jostled by a moving mass of disgruntled travelers. But for what seemed like an eternity he looked only at her. Then, taking two steps forward, he cupped her face between his hands. Just before he stamped his mouth over hers, he growled, "God, yes."

CHAPTER 10

It looks like a maze," Laney observed, looking down at Deke's improvisation.

"Let's just hope they can't find their way out," he said laughingly. He had arranged bolster pillows around the perimeter of the bed in the guest bedroom of his apartment. Then he had placed one horizontally across the bed. A twin was on either side of the center pillow. "Even the threat of picket lines and terrorist activities in the store wouldn't induce Macy's to deliver two baby beds today." He pinched his wife's bottom. "Give me more notice next time."

"Oh, coming from you, that's laughable. You've never notified anyone that you were about to mow them down, have you?"

"What would you have done if I'd called you up one night and said, 'Hello, Ms. McLeod, you may not remember me. I'm the guy who rescued you during the blackout. I took you to my apartment. You took off all your clothes, got in my bed and I taught you how to—"

"I'd have hung up immediately."

" '—and I was just wondering if you'd ever like to engage in that kind of licentious activity again.' " His voice dropped seductively. "Sometime. Whenever you're free. Like right now." For the first time since she'd known him, Laney detected an element of shyness in the man whose well of self-confidence she had thought would never run dry. "Did . . . did you see Dr. Taylor, uh, before you left?"

She plucked at a button on his shirt. "Uh-huh."

He swallowed hard. "And?"

Coyly she raised her chin and let her eyes tell him what he wanted to know.

He didn't give her time to expound. His hands splayed over her back and pressed her willing body to his. Confidence restored, his mouth had its way with hers, with the arrogance of a warlord who claims the village virgin. His fervor cooled only long enough to lift her in his arms and carry her into the bedroom they had shared once before. When he set her on her feet, he gathered her close for another breath-stealing kiss.

"I can't believe this is happening to me." Her mouth fluttered over his neck as his lips drew a path of kisses to her ear.

"Believe it. Believe that I love you with all my heart and am going to spend every day of my life telling you how much you mean to me." Her face was worshiped by emerald eyes. "You're gorgeous, Mrs. Sargent. I always did like that suit."

"I didn't think you'd noticed." She was wearing the suit she had worn the night they met. Until today it had hung in her closet.

"I noticed." He eased her jacket from her shoulders and down her arms. "I didn't have the privilege of undressing you before."

"Nor I you." She ran her hands over his lapels before she slipped his suit jacket down his arms.

During the blackout in the elevator, he had fumbled to untie the scarf around her neck. Now he caught it with deft fingers and methodically unwound it at his leisure. She worked with equal concentration on his necktie. At the same time, staring into each other's eyes, they pulled shirttails from waistbands. Her blouse came off only moments before she dropped his shirt to the floor.

Soft words of adoration came from his lips as his eyes wandered over her breasts. She was wearing the same bra she had worn that night. The glossy, sheer blue fabric was under stress to contain her breasts, which were fuller now. Creamy flesh swelled above the lacy border. His finger drifted across that satiny expanse.

She laid her hands on his chest and when she felt his breath quicken, she glanced up at him inquiringly. "Go ahead," he murmured. "Do whatever feels right. And only because you want to. Not because you think I expect it."

Her hands combed through the mat of dark hair sprinkled here and there with silver. Acting on impulse and hunger for him, she leaned forward and brushed her lips across the crinkly hair. Then she stayed to kiss the suntanned flesh beneath, her tongue flicking across his nipples.

"God, Laney. You're killing me."

He worked free the fastener of her brassiere and pulled it away from her body. She shimmied out of it. His breath was stopped momentarily as he gazed down on her breasts. Then he placed his hands at the small of her back, arched her over and hotly planted his mouth at the base of her throat. Groaning his pleasure, he kissed his way down her chest, over the lushness of her breasts to the tight bead of one nipple.

"Deke . . ." That thread of a sigh escaped her as his lips kissed her sweetly, from one breast to the other. His tongue was a quick, wet tormentor that coaxed the dusky areolas to shrink and pout and thrust their crowns between his eager lips.

His hard maleness found the cove of her womanhood and secured itself there, rubbing against her with erotic undulations. She chanted his name like a pagan litany as her fingers tangled in his hair.

On the brink of losing all control, he kissed his way up and found her mouth to be as eager as his. "I swear to you, one day soon, we'll play this doctor game all afternoon, but right now . . . ah, Laney . . . I'm just too hungry for you."

With fumbling fingers he unsnapped and unzipped her skirt. Gathering it and her slip and pantyhose in one gentle fist, he dragged the garments down her legs as he dropped to his knees in front of her. "Look at you," he whispered adoringly as she stepped out of the garments. His hands coasted over her as though he were afraid to spoil her ethereal beauty with his carnal touch. He softly kissed each side of her recently slenderized waist, her flattened stomach, the dimple of her navel, the lavish nest of tawny hair, the tops of her thighs.

She whimpered and swayed toward him.

He stood and clutched her tightly, bringing both her arms up around his neck. "Hold on. We're almost there." He reached for his belt. There was the clink of metal, the sibilance of leather and cloth rubbing together, the sound of a zipper. The backs of his fingers, as they accomplished those infuriatingly necessary tasks, were kneading her belly. He stepped out of his shoes and, not releasing her, stretched down to peel off his socks. Then he let the trousers fall, and nothing separated them but the stretched white cloth of his briefs.

Her breathing was rapid and warm as it fell on his chest, stirring the hair. Her head was shyly bowed and he could feel the tension in her body. "It's all right, Laney. I know it's been a long time. We can stop anytime you say." His voice was gentle and she loved him for it.

"No. I want you. I want to touch you."

Resting her forehead on the sturdy muscles of his chest, she let one hand glide down his torso. From shoulder to chest, over the corded tautness of his stomach, her fingers meandered down. He held his breath in suspense, but it rushed out in a low, ragged moan when she peeled the underwear down and closed her hand around his proud sex.

"My love, my love." He lifted her against him and carried her to the bed. They were as one, fused together as he lowered her to the linens.

The kiss went on and on. They explored each other's mouths as they relished the feel, the splendor, of their nakedness. Then slowly he lifted his lips from hers. Moving down her body, he paid it tribute. A score of kisses were left on her throat. With his teeth he nipped the tender undersides of her upper arms, the sides of her breasts. His tongue plundered the responsive insides of her elbows. He acquainted her with every erogenous spot of her body.

Her breasts were honored by gently caressing fingertips and lips. His tongue bathed their peaked crests lovingly, delicately, maddeningly. He kissed each rib, her stomach, her belly. Her navel was debauched by a wickedly hedonistic tongue. It repeatedly glanced the tops of her thighs, then languished in the shallow grooves that funneled toward the center of her heat.

"I love you."

The words reached her ears just as she felt his mouth blessing her with the most intimate caress. She swirled in a maelstrom of ecstasy, her passions as undisciplined as the liberties he took. With loving lips he expressed his love, then his unbridled tongue stoked the fires of her desire until her body could no longer contain them and she began to tremble. He knew she was ready to receive him and levered himself above her.

"Tell me if I hurt you."

Their eyes met and transmitted a thousand messages of love as his body sank into hers. "Don't hold back,

Deke," she pleaded, and curled her limbs around him to bring him securely into her body.

He breathed curses and prayers into her ear as her wet silkiness swallowed all of him and entrapped him in the sweetest haven he had ever known. "Laney, it's beautiful, isn't it?"

"Yes, beautiful. Just as I remember. Only finer. Much finer."

He gave himself up to it then and let their senses guide them. They matched movements and tempos perfectly. With each stroke their souls as well as their bodies were enriched. When the tumult came, they clung to each other, laughing, crying. Like a healing potion, his love burst into her, exorcising any trace of fear and imbuing her with the assurance that she was loved.

"I forgot to ask. How is the trial going?" Laney idly examined the intricacies of Deke's chest. She tweaked clumps of springy hair between curious fingers.

After lying in the languorous aftermath of love for a long while, they had eventually stirred and gone to check on the twins, who were sleeping soundly in spite of their new environment. When Deke remarked that it would soon be time for the two-o'clock feeding, Laney told him they were now sleeping through the night. They had returned to their bed to contentedly cuddle. Deke was propped on the pillows in a half-sitting position against the headboard. Laney lay between his legs, her breasts filling the hollow beneath his rib cage.

"We got a verdict shortly after noon today."

"No doubt you won."

His smile was crooked and a trifle chagrined. "Not exactly. He was found guilty of having sticky fingers in the company's till, but he got off with a stiff fine and a five-year probation. I protested the verdict, of course, but I was pleased."

"Was he guilty?"

His grin was deliciously satanical. "As hell."

She laughed and snuggled against him. "You're incorrigible."

"But you love me?" There was no avoiding the questioning.

Her eyes were clear with love and free of the sadness that had always clouded them. "Yes. I love you."

"I was leading the witness."

She crawled up his body to place her lips against his. "I love you. And I would swear it under oath."

She kissed him and he delighted in her lack of inhibition. His hands traveled down her back and over the gentle swelling of her derriere. He was rewarded by a purr of reawakened arousal. But there were things he wanted to tell her, so he lifted his mouth, and his hands sought the more neutral territory of her shoulders.

"Tomorrow you'll meet my family."

Her head came up. "Deke, so soon?"

"It's my mother's birthday dinner. A family tradition—the gathering of the clan." He tried to make light of it.

"You can go without us."

Her anguish was real and he knew it. "My mother would never speak to me again. She thinks I planned your arrival with the twins for her present. And since I've been caught up in the trial and haven't shopped for anything else, you've saved my neck."

When he could see that she was still concerned, he drew her close and pressed his mouth to her forehead. "Laney, I'm very proud that you're my wife. I want to share you with my family and them with you. They can't wait to meet you. You'll be stuffed with food, drowned with drink, kissed by cousins, hugged by everyone. You won't be able to work a word in edge-wise, and there will be tribal warfare over who gets to hold the twins. I promise."

Her eyes misted as she smiled. Never having known the kind of happy confusion that goes with a large fam-ily gathering, she thought it sounded too good to be true. "I'm scared. But it sounds wonderful."

"You're wonderful." He kissed her, guaranteeing with his ardor that, as with all his promises, this one would come true as well. Her response stirred him, but he wanted all the corners of their new life swept clear of debris.

"I've looked at a house," he began.

She shook her head, sweeping his massaging hands with her hair. Unconsciously everything she did now was sensuous, sexual. She had been wrapped in a chrysalis of unhappiness and insecurity. But under Deke's gentle coaching she had thrown off that cocoon of self-consciousness to become a woman capable of both giving and accepting great passion. She had found self-confidence in his love for her.

"That's not necessary, Deke, honestly it isn't. When

I was objecting to living here, it wasn't because of the location." She looked up at him impishly. "Besides, I have friends just a few floors up. Remember Sally and Jeff? I guess I should call and tell them that I'm married and living here now."

"I want to meet them, too, but don't call right now." He took her mouth under his for a long, slow kiss that was as deep and probing and thorough as his lovemaking. When he drew back, he toyed with the strands of hair that framed her face. "Back to the topic of houses. I know you don't care for high-rises because of the elevators." He playfully tugged on a honey-blond curl. "And I don't want my children to grow up without a huge yard to romp in. I've found a house that I hope meets with your approval."

"If you're sure that's what you want to do, Deke." Inching herself down again, she whisked light kisses over his torso as she went. Her hands were never still.

"It is. This is a bachelor pad. Not a family dwelling."

Hearing him say that made her inordinately pleased. She rubbed his abdomen with her nose, her chin, her lips, nuzzling him. "We should decide on something soon. Right now we have three residences."

"What do you want to do with the house in Sunnyvale? I'll buy it if you want me to." For what she was doing to him, he would have done anything she wanted him to. "You might want to know it's there to go back to."

She laid her cheek on his thigh and let her hands run up and down the muscled columns of his legs. Her voice was quiet. "There won't be any going back."

"Laney," he groaned when her tongue touched him ever so lightly. He pulled her up to lie on his chest so he could look directly into her eyes. "I can't tell you how happy it makes me to hear you say that."

"I can't tell you how happy I am."

They kissed and it was a covenant, more binding than a marriage license or spoken vow. His arms closed around her. Once more in repose, her eyes wandered around the room. "That morning when I sneaked out, I would never have imagined that I'd be back, like this, doing this."

Mischievously she let her middle roll against his. But it was she who was surprised when she felt his hard readiness plowing into her stomach. His eyes flashed, but his hands were gentle as they skimmed down the backs of her thighs, parted them, caressed. He lifted her hips over him.

Her eyes became dark and smoky with passion. The pulse in her throat throbbed against his searching lips. "I thought you would forget me as soon as I left, Deke. Why did you care enough to come looking for me?"

His breath faltered as she took him gradually, slowly but inexorably, accepting him into the moist mystery of her body. "I knew I'd found the woman I wanted to share my life with." His thumbs rotated over the points of her pelvic bones and his fingers curved around to sink into the flesh of her hips and hold her fast. Her body sinuously rocked over his. "None other would do. None had. I wanted you in my life and I had to find you. I *had* to. My, God, Laney . . . ah, sweet . . ."

His body strained upward, reaching to touch her

womb. He leaned forward and, palming her breast, lifted it to his mouth. Her head fell back as he closed his lips around her nipple. His surging motions deep inside her drove her closer and closer toward the sublime.

It rushed upon them and smothered them in its golden warmth. Their veins throbbed with pleasure. Their senses hummed with fulfillment. Their spirits were forged together with a heat so intense it would burn forever.

"Deke, are you asleep?"

"Uh-huh."

"Do you know what today is?"

"Uh-huh. Saturday."

"No, I mean the date."

He rolled onto his stomach, propped himself on his elbows and looked at her. They were having a picnic lunch on the parklike grounds surrounding the stately Tudor house they had purchased. Laney and Deke were sharing one blanket while the twins were sharing another. All were enjoying the drowsy sunshine of an early-summer day.

They had made a trip to Arkansas to settle their affairs. The lease to the house had been turned back over to the landlady. Most of the furniture had been given away. Only a few pieces had been shipped to New York. The station wagon had been given to a flabbergasted Mrs. Thomas. Laney had declined the contract Mr. Harper offered.

But no sooner had they moved into their house than

she had secured a position with the elementary school nearest them. Starting with the fall semester, she would act as a teacher's aide, working only a few hours each morning. Deke had endorsed her decision completely, realizing that he never wanted her to feel trapped, insulated, smothered. It was no wonder to him that she was claustrophobic. She had grown up in four walls surrounding a lifeless, emotionally suffocating atmosphere. He would always give her freedom, yet wrap her in love.

"The date?" he asked now, catching her around her bare ankle and massaging the sensitive spot with a decadent thumb.

The muscles of her leg twitched. "Stop, Deke, I have something to say."

"So do I. You have outrageously sexy ankles." He twisted an imaginary villain's mustache. "And other sexy things as well, and I have a lech for you that won't quit." He caught her Achilles tendon between his teeth. "Wanna make love out here under the trees?"

His hand slid under her jean leg to squeeze her calf. She didn't draw her foot away, but he could see that something else was on her mind. He withdrew his hand. "What did you want to tell me?" he asked seriously. Sometimes his sensitivity to her moods was uncanny. That was only one of the reasons she loved him.

"It's our anniversary. It was a year ago today that we met in that elevator during the blackout."

"I hadn't even thought of that," he said, sitting up.

"I have a present for you." She took a gift-wrapped box out of the picnic basket and handed it to him. "I'm not sure you'll like it."

He watched her for an endless minute and she recognized that look. On several occasions he had invited her to be a spectator in the courtroom. His demand for the truth from a witness was unrelenting. Between probing questions Deke would watch the witness long and hard as though piercing through his defenses and reading his innermost thoughts. If the witness were lying, he invariably squirmed under that incisive gaze. Laney didn't. What she had said wasn't just rhetorical. She really was afraid he wouldn't like her gift.

Deke unwrapped the package. Without speaking he opened the jeweler's box and saw the gold wedding band secured in its velvet lining.

"You don't have to wear it if you don't want to," she said softly, nervously. "But I didn't bring anything into our marriage. Not even a wedding ring for you."

Her heart stopped when he handed the box back to her. But then she saw his eyes and they were glassy with emotion. "Put it on me, please."

Taking the ring from the box, she slipped it on his ring finger. He clasped her hand tightly. "How can you say you brought nothing to the marriage? You *are* the marriage." He moved across the blanket and folded his hands around her head, linking his fingers in the back. He drew her mouth beneath his and their tongues exchanged intimacies.

"I was going to wait until we went out to dinner tonight, but . . ." He took a box from his jacket pocket and handed it to her.

"Oh, you!" she exclaimed, wiping tears of love from her eyes. "You remembered all along."

"How could I forget the most momentous day of my life?" She tossed away the wrapping paper and found another jeweler's box, this one long, slender and flat. Lying golden and beautiful on a white satin lining was a smooth oval locket on a long chain.

Reverently, Laney lifted it out and sprung the delicate hinge open. In one of the tiny frames was a reduced picture of her and Deke taken by one of his brothers at a recent family get-together. They were smiling radiantly, their heads close, their happiness with each other enviable. In the other frame was a picture of the twins lying side by side in three-month-old perfection.

Laney couldn't speak for the tentacles of emotion that squeezed her throat. "It's inscribed," Deke said quietly. On the back was engraved, *Our family, our love. Your Deke.* Taking the locket from her shaking fingers, he slipped it over her head and watched it nestle between her breasts.

She lifted the locket to her lips and kissed it, then pressed it back onto the setting it seemed made for. "I love you so much it hurts sometimes."

This time, when their mouths met, their bodies did as well. They reclined together on the blanket. His hand slipped under her cotton sweater and found her braless breasts full and warm and vibrant with love. He pushed her sweater up and gazed at the patterns of sunlight and shadow that danced across them. He lowered his head and let his lips drift over them as lightly and lazily as the sunbeams.

"Deke, we can't. The staff—"

"Has the afternoon off, remember?"

"The babies?" Her voice had lost some of its impetus as a result of the agile tongue that circled her nipples.

"Couldn't care less."

They looked at the infants curled up together. They had filled out and were plump and rosy, a testimony to the happy atmosphere that surrounded them. "They're precious, aren't they?" Laney said softly.

"Yes. You know, it's curious. Every time there's a blackout in the city, there is a baby boom nine months later. I didn't hear anything about one this time. But then the blackout only lasted about ten minutes."

Laney's naughty laugh brought her husband's attention back to her. Her mouth rubbed invitingly against his. "Then you're a ten-minute wonder. In that amount of time we certainly did our share to promote a baby boom."

His grin was the rakish, overconfident one that she adored. He worked his hand between them and unzipped first her jeans, then his. Willingly she let him adjust their clothing. Heartbeats later she felt his virility, hard and velvety warm, moving against her, seeking. "Haven't I always told you that I'm a man who gets quick results?"

She had to admit that he was, since he found her warm and moist and swollen with desire for his loving.

"Laney. My dearest, dearest love."

And he always knew the right words to say.